AF191955

ELEONORA GEORGETA BULZ

BEFORE DEATH

novum pro

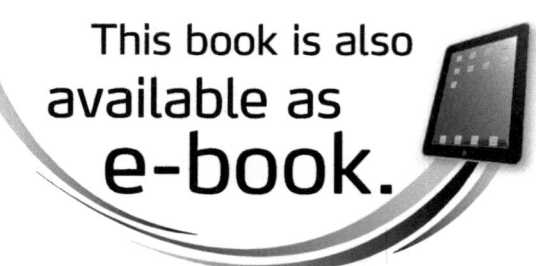

This book is also
available as
e-book.

www.novum-publishing.co.uk

© 2022 novum publishing

ISBN 978-3-99131-358-8
Editing: Nicola Grün
Cover photos: Yufa12379, Aivolie,
Captblack76 | Dreamstime.com
Cover design, layout & typesetting:
novum publishing

www.novum-publishing.co.uk

Climate neutral
Print product
ClimatePartner.com/16547-2201-1002

When she got off the plane, Magi realised that she had entered a special and different world. If during the nine-hour flight she tried to encourage herself, now, in the middle of the crowd, she felt alone, without the support and the safety of the place she got used to for a lifetime. What was waiting for her in this new world, in the new position she had chosen as a nanny? No, nobody obliged her to come here, except that she had to earn money in order to have a better living.

In her native country, after the communism collapsed and its replacement by a kind of ferocious demo-communism, a real rush for getting rich was unbridled, through economic destruction, plunder, and theft legalized by the new leaders, the so-called democrats. In those years, many people left the country to work illegally in the developed countries, otherwise, they would have risked not surviving. Hope for a better life turned into disbelief and despair. After many years of leaving herself to her fate, in a moment of despair that seemed to be extraordinary luck, she accepted to be a nanny for a family in the Land of Promise. She could speak the language, she had a driving license, and a huge desire to get rid of poverty. So, here she was, passing through the crowd, looking for a person who had her name written on a piece of cardboard.

'I think you are waiting for me. Hello!'

'Hello, Magi, and welcome. I thought I had lost you.'

'It took some time until my luggage arrived.'

'I am Lucy, the mother of the two children you came for.'

Dragging her luggage, Magi managed to get to the car. During the journey, Magi watched her new boss closely. She was around 30 years old. She looked tired but she was like a chatter box, trying to tell Magi some of the secrets of her new job. A hooked nose that arouse suspicion,, two big eyes that looked like they were hypnotising you, and a pretty sensual mouth with a sinister smile that seemed to give you the creeps. Lucy's brown hair with reddish hues was kept tight around her head, only a few locks of hair fell on her forehead and at the back of her head. With an average height and harmonious body, Lucy seemed like the ideal type of mother and wife. Magi congratulated herself for the choice she had made, confident that finally, she was in the right place at the right time.

Three hours later, they arrived in front of the house but Magi had not realised how the time had passed because she was focused on the future duties that were waiting for her. Because it was evening, all she could see was an isolated house with two floors and a garage. It looked terrifying, bleak, cold, and threatening and the trees around it looked like a shield. It looked like a house out of a fairy tale. They entered directly into the dining room and Lucy invited Magi to go downstairs and see her room with a large smile.

'We have the basement arranged as a flat. I thought you would feel better and safer here. You have everything you need here, TV, toilet, shower. You can enjoy all the privacy you need. Of course, we have the laundry here and my husband's small workshop. He is fond of inquisition, medieval prisons and all sorts of devices designed, as he says, for relaxation through suffering. He is a good and understanding man, anyway.'

Magi felt a chill of fear down her spine but as she watched Lucy's warm and smiling face, she put aside any kind of ill omen.

'Where are the kids?'

Magi asked her, bewildered by the silence of the house.

'They spend a lot of time with their grandparents during school time because, you see, our house is far away and I am sure you will find it hard to drive to at the beginning. You will have some time to get used to the house, to us, and the surroundings. Do not worry, you will have plenty to do even if they are not here… I will leave you alone now and when you are ready, come upstairs and meet my husband and see the rest of the house if you are not too tired.'

Finally alone, Magi noticed that the room that was pretty spacious. There was a double bed in the middle with two nightstands on each side and a bed lamp on each. On the opposite side, there was a chest of drawers with many drawers, a cable TV set on it, and beside it a large lumber-room with many pegs and shelves. Everything was simple and functional. She saw the window attached to a kind of ventilation and she felt the air coming from somewhere above where the light was coming through. She was disappointed by this fake window because she thought she could take in the forest at night. The bathroom was a few meters from the room door down a long corridor where two washing machines were placed and a door led to Lucy's husband's workshop.

Magi would have liked her bathroom next to her room but she could not have the least pretension. After she had arranged a part of her things in the lumber-room and the drawer, luckily there were not so many things, she thought of taking a shower because she was very tired and had to freshen up a little. The bathroom was small but the shower, the toilet, and the sink did not take too much space, there was space enough to move. What impressed her most was the mirror that took up half of the wall and gave the impression of a window. Everything was bright, the beige tiles with brown spots made one feel fresh and hopeful. However, a strange feeling made her feel awkward about her nudity as if she wanted to draw a curtain over the mirror.

'God, do not let me feel so suspicious, it is nothing but a mirror and if you do not like your body, do not watch. I took a shower letting myself be caressed by the water stream. I was content at that moment, happy to have taken this step and hopeful that everything was going to be fine. Nothing bad could happen to me.'

Feeling refreshed, Magi put on a pretty large dress, the kind that lets nothing be seen through and hoped to please her future masters.

The stairs led to a corridor behind the house a door opened into the main house. The hall was bright with stairs leading to the two floors and the kitchen was in front. Magi was guided by the noises and she entered a large kitchen, the kind that she had seen only in movies, which connected to a living room that was decorated in good taste and was extremely elegant.

'I was just cooking something. You must be hungry and tired. My husband has not finished his job yet so it is only the two of us.'

'I can help you, just tell me what to do.'

'Today I want to spoil you because you start your job tomorrow but I will be around you till you learn. In one week at the most you will feel at home.'

Because Magi was rather hungry, she ate the piece of dough filled with something that seemed like meat, cheese, and tomato juice cooked in the microwave really fast.

'We eat something like this but if you want to cook, tell me to buy what you like.'

'Thanks, but it is not worth cooking for one person, so I will eat what you do.'

'As if you are coming from another world. You know, when we tried to find a nanny, my husband strongly wanted to know her name. He says the name always defines the person. He was very surprised by your name and was convinced it would be an extraordinary challenge to have around a nanny with such a strange name. He said she had to have a very strong personality and this excites him. However, you will have time to meet him because I wanted a nanny for at least one year. I will clean up here so good night and sweet dreams in your new home.'

The way Lucy had said the last part, "sweet dreams" seemed so strange to Magi especially because she watched her for so long in an interesting way. Magi was very tired so she started towards her room. When she arrived in front of the workshop, she heard noises of ironmongery. Her attention was drawn towardhis passion for strange things. It was not her business, after all, everyone has their own hobby.

THE DREAM

Magi fell into such a deep sleep as if a force was pulling her towards it, not to harm her but to send her a message, to teach her something she was supposed to have known for so long, that was lost together with the last sorcerer. An old man appeared with his eyebrows united. Magi was in an alley inher country and using signs, he urged her to enter the courtyard of a house. He was ill, he was in pain but every time he tried to close his eyes to have a rest, something forced him to stay awake. Magi was scared by the way he was begging her to enter that yard, his eyes were telling her that she had to do what she was told, that only this way she would hear his message. She felt paralysed, her feet did not listen to her as if they were stuck on the ground. She felt the desperation in the old man's eyes as if wanting to help her get unstuck but his powers were diminishing...

She closed her eyes and tried to think about light. She saw her grandfather passing her by and touching her with his kindness, whispering in her mind. 'You must do it, only you can help the sorcerer, before death...'

It was something dark that did not let her reach there, she tried to yell but a pair of tongs was squeezing her throat and she slowly began to choke.

Magi woke up drenched in sweat and feeling like she could not breathe. She still felt the pressure of the metal on her chest. The air in the room seemed heavy, a smell of horror, of suffering... Then she reminded the sorcerer. It seemed as though she had not dreamt and he was waiting for her to enter that courtyard but something was hindering her, maybe the air, the smell...

When Magi recovered, she thought it was only a dream, the new house, the new room, new bed. That must have been it, this period would pass too. She looked at the watch which read 6:30 so it was useless to go back to sleep. She inspected the room again, this time more relaxed, and she noticed some new things.

One mirror was in every corner, arranged so that the whole room could be seen. She looked out of the window and saw a metal ladder one meter away from the ground that led up to the top where a glass roof stretched with some empty spaces where the air could enter. The room was cool because of the air conditioner but she was grateful it existed and thought maybe one night she would climb up the roof and watch the silence of the night.

One hour later, she decided she could go upstairs without disturbing anybody. When she reached the corridor at the back of the house, she saw a door that looked out on the yard so she decided to go out and get some fresh air. When Magi opened it, she reached a terrace in what seemed like another realm. The supporting pillars were covered in ivy and climbing roses. The feeling of entering a world of colors and smells flooded her. A few rocking chairs and small tables seemed to be waiting for their guests. All around the grass was tall, weaving with the field flowers, wild roses, and thorns amongst which a few lanes wound. A few meters away the forest began, trembling at each wind blow, like a sigh coming from the earth's being. Overwhelmed, Magi slipped into the rocking chair but a hand caught her shoulder. She panicked and the spellbound broke.

'Good morning. I apologise for not meeting you last night but I am so passionate about my hobby that I could forget to eat if Lucy did not bring me some food. My name is Fer and I hope we will get on well together. In fact, you will see only a little of me so I am sure we will get on well together.'

The resemblance between the two of them was so obvious that Magi was stunned. He was taller and his eyes looked like copper in the sunlight. He had a strange beauty, something warned me not to stay defenseless but Magi could hardly move in his presence.

'I can see how amased you are by the resemblance between me and Lucy. You are right but they say that when couples have many things in common, sometimes they start with physical resemblance. I think the two of us have something in common. Glad to meet you, I will leave you in Lucy's company.'

Without waiting for her reply, he turned his back and left. Magi was too troubled by this appearance so she remained still in the rocking chair. Suddenly, she felt the same smell in the room that she smelled when she woke up from her dream. It was the smell of horror and suffering. And then she saw the sorcerer pleading with her to enter the yard.

'Hey... I can see you woke up early and discovered the paradise. This place looks like a mystery, something beyond death. If you want to eat something or drink a cup of coffee, come with me to the kitchen to show you where the world starts.

I followed her still under the powerful impression of what I had seen. I was like in a dream where the sublime mingles with pain, a place that urges you to stay but also warns you to run away.'

'Everything starts in the kitchen, all the domestic appliances come to life in skillful hands but they can also bring destruction.'

Lucy started to show Magi how the coffee maker and the dishwasher worked, everything that belonged to a fully-equipped kitchen. After Magi ate something and drank a cup of coffee, Lucy showed her the house.

'You are familiar with the basement already so we shall start on the second floor. This belongs to my husband with a bedroom, a study, a small room for meditation that looks onto a terrace where you have a view of the whole estate. You must come here only when I tell you to because Fer likes to be isolated. That is why he has a kitchen here too. There is a bathroom next to his bedroom and another door that goes to a secret room where nobody else is allowed. On the first floor, there are three bedrooms in an old style, beds with canopy, all with bathrooms, and one is occupied by me.'

Magi was surprised she did not see the children's rooms but maybe they did not need them because they spent most of the time with their grandparents. There should be some little things belonging to them in case they came home. It was natural to ask herself why they needed a nanny. Magi left this question for some other time, convinced there was an explanation. So far, she realized that her work would be that of a housekeeper.

'As long as we are without kids, you will be a housekeeper, I hope you do not mind that. It is not hard at all especially as there is nobody to make dirt. You will enter the bedrooms every day. In mine, you will make the bed and clean the bathroom. As for the rest you will dust the furniture and keep everything clean.'

'I do not find it difficult at all, on the contrary, I feel it is too little to do.'

'I do not want you to have much to do, a little but good quality, that is my slogan. By the way, once a week you have to vacuum the whole house and on another day you will have to do all the laundry you find in the baskets in our rooms. Yours, when you program it. I hope I did not scare you but if you make a program things go easier. Today you can start on the second floor because Fer will be gone for a while. In the morning when you wake up, you can make coffee and eat what you want, because I never know what I shall eat so I will not put another burden on you.'

The first day passed quickly and focused on her work, Lucy did not realise when the evening fell. She was alone most of the day. She cooked something and went out on the mysterious terrace that sent her into another world. It was so quiet in that rustle of nature, Magi felt closed and free at the same time as if she got swept up in the flower petals that blew in the wind among the trees. Magi forgot about myself, her eyes closed and she fell asleep like a log.

'Because you were born under the sign of Magic, only you can defeat the Evil.'

'But I cannot see any evil anywhere!'

'Not yet, not yet, the time has not come yet… But when it comes, you must be ready, otherwise, another life will be lost…'

'Who is the sorcerer and what does he want from me?'

'He is the sorcerer that died and still, he is before death, he is not received in the afterlife until he transmits the magic spell. We, the Great, that will help you face the Evil.'

Horrified, Magi wanted to answer him but somebody was shaking her so hard that she woke up.

'I am glad you woke up because you were tossing in your sleep and speaking to somebody in your language. Maybe the position and the fatigue are the cause. I know the place is wonderful but it is not good to sleep in the rocking chair. Good night and sweeter dreams.'

Although Lucy was trying to hide it, Magi felt a little anger and discontent in her voice for what had happened. Maybe Lucy did not like the fact Magi had fallen asleep on the terrace or maybe it was Lucy's refuge and she felt Magi had invaded it. Magi would be more attentive in the future, she said to myself and she left for my room, thinking about the shower she was going to take.

Once in her room, Lucy was as nervous as hell. She was dropping things everywhere, kicking everything in her way.

'The whore, she found the place to sleep, on the spot where the spirits of good are strong and can not reach her. They may show themselves in her sleep and help her. I must keep her away from this place as much as I can, to find all my powers to destroy the sign of magic.

The big eyes looked like two light spheres, her nose as a prayer beak, and horror sounds of fury came out of her large open mouth. Then, stricken by panic, she ran to find Fer. She felt that he was attracted to this human being and she wanted to keep an eye on her, now in the 12ᵗʰ hour. No, she would not let happen to him exactly what had happened to their father. She was the force, the engine of revenge, but this time without his help she would not be able to fight against corrupters, she was the root that needed to be pulled out and burned. "She is the weakness and the most harmful vice, mercy.""

She found him in his refuge on the second floor, smoking a cigarette. Suddenly she became all milk and honey. All these years she had been taking care of him, she learned that she could master him only with kindness. Any time she let herself be controlled by fury in front of him, he fell into a trance, retreated into his shell and it took days until she succeeded to take him back. Each time she had to remind him what had happened to their father, what kind of a demon lies in these Eves, their touch meaning death and she could not lose another dear man.

Without watching her, Fer asked:

'Did you come to verify your creation?'
    Sometimes he could be very sarcastic but she did not pay attention, used to his whims.

'You know you mean everything to me, you are my universe, my desire to exist is you. I fought for you, I protected you and kept away from all that vice, weakness, mercy, love. Love is nothing but the evil you do to yourself, the fruit you tasted and takes you to perdition.'

'Then why do you love me? Aren't you afraid that this love leads to perdition?'

'I am afraid, indeed, and I often think what if I would leave you alone to face all these but I hear our father asking for revenge. He asks me not to leave you even if I have to pay the ultimate price. I refused love because I could not watch weakness. Virtue

15

is nothing but our invention, we hide our weakness and vices behind it. The joy that virtue gives weakens the human race.'

'And your love for me ... What is its name?'

'At least that is what I have learned, nobody is perfect and my love proves it. My love might be my perish but I must assume it. As long as you do not oppose me I have a free way.'

'I stopped opposing a long time ago, especially because you keep reminding me that you had saved me.'

'As long as you remember it we are both safe. About the new nanny, I watched her taking a shower and then in the room. If you have not done it so far it means that either you are not attracted to her or you are attracted too much so and it is not good. I arranged these mirrors so that you can enjoy them without touching them. Why do not you open the mirror to see her?'

She wanted to observe him while he was watching her to see if she was going to have problems in the future when she decides her fate. It is exactly what happened to one of them to who he became too attached. She had an angelic beauty, you could reproach nothing except her naivety and trust. The perfect type that men raise to the level of a goddess and dedicate altars to. She was from a far away country, a young girl of 21. Her relatives announced that she had married but her husband accepted nobody in the family but she sent them some money, a pretty large sum and that was all. That is what money meant – power.

'I can understand why you refuse to watch her. Of course, she is not as beautiful as others but she has got something that sets you on fire. Her obedience is suspicious and her eyes, I have never seen such eyes in my life. As dark as pitch, you cannot penetrate beyond, as if they are a kind of barrier.'

'Sometimes I think that all you do, you do more for yourself, and I am just an excuse for your sickness, one that makes you feel better.'

'Don't you dare tell me such a thing, ever!'

She cried furiously but the next second she embraced him and apologised. Reluctantly, he answered because he knew the power of her hatred and wanted to get rid of her as soon as possible.

Intuiting that he wanted to get rid of her, Lucy left wishing him good night. She still had a lot to do that night, to clean up the place from the last torture, to inject the two victims with drugs to make them unaware of what was going to happen and keep the, quiet while being horrified by what they saw. Sleep for her was like torture, she could not forget anything, not even in her sleep. She tried to use sleeping pills but it did not work, the only help were the drugs, they made her forget all the suffering. However, she had to sleep from time to time but she tried to postpone it as much as possible. Any moment of relaxation meant memories that would haunt her and strengthen her until death. She would give back all she had received because only this way she could get rid of the demon. Some would say she was sick, the way her brother did sometimes, but she knew this illness was given to her in all the years of suffering she had to endure for two human beings. As her step mother liked to say: If you want us not to bother your brother, you must suffer twice + 1, once for you, once for your brother and once only for my pleasure. Even now she could remember the first night she sneaked into her bed. She was 13, with a very rich father but totally helpless in front to woman. A year after her mother's death, when she first came to their house as a nanny, she looked like any other woman, obeying, loving, and ready to fulfill any of their wishes. But she never liked her gray eyes that were inspecting everything, wishing to be in 100 places at the same time.

Extremely modest, when she realized she was accepted by the family, she started to become more aware of her looks. Her skirts became shorter and shorter, her neck openings of her dresses bigger and bigger and she started to treat her father with more attention and kindness. She started to wait for him late at night to tell him what they had done that day, to ask for advice about her life, to tell him how lonely she was and how much she loved the kids. Especially Fer, who had always been a sick child, retired and shy, and with whom she spent a lot of time, trying to give him back his self-confidence. It was a time when she had a woman who used to come three times a week to clean and cook but she convinced him to let her do everything. And so, step by step, she isolated the kids and made them depend on her. But Lucy was watching and understood everything and she tried a few times to warn her father but he rejected her saying it was all her fantasy and jealousy. Her father, an old man of 59 and old-fashioned, had a nice relationship with her mother. He was the only child, inheriting a large fortune. Lucy's mother had one more sister who never married because she was rather sick. Her mother's family was not as rich as her father's but they were well-off so 10 years ago, when her aunt died, they found themselves richer. It was her father's richness and weak personality that attracted their nanny, realising that he was going to be only a toy in her hands. The nanny had no problems with Fer being so weak and sick so he was no danger. It was only Lucy who was in her way. The nanny manipulated her father so well that he saw only the jealousy of a little girl who wanted to keep her father for herself and did not want to give up her mother's place in her warning attempts.

The nanny was so affectionate towards her in her father's presence and no matter how hard she tried to make her reveal her inner truth, the nanny responded with more affection and understanding. At that time and at her age, she did not realise she was wrong but she could not understand why an adult could not see the truth. When they were at home alone, the nanny used to tell her that her revenge would be cruel and she should get ready for the worst but she have never imagined that she could bear so much.

After marriage, a happy period followed. The nanny seemed to have forgotten everything the moment she reached her goal but Lucy did not know it was not that way and she prayed every night for her father to protect them from bad things. He used to go away on business for long periods and she hoped a new nanny was coming for Fer but when she asked her stepmother, she answered:

'It is time he recovered, finally, he is 7 years old and has not a bit of self-confidence. He was too spoiled and he has always been told he was ill and so he ended up believing it. If he needs more attention it is you who will take care of him, I have had enough.'

So Lucy started to spend more time with Fer to encourage him. She thought his illness was caused more by his kind and shy nature. Even if he was an intelligent child, his shyness caused many awkward situations. He was so shy that sometimes he was speechless and had no voice to answer the questions in the classroom. He had confessed that when a teacher used to ask him a question his heart seemed to stop and his head turned to the back. The other children laughed at him and this made him retreat even more. Lucy tried to convince him he was intelligent because he used to read so many books they had in the house. She explained to him that everything was inside him and if he succeeded to defeat his shyness, he could be brilliant. Slowly he started to trust himself and succeeded to be among the top of his class. It meant a lot of nervous effort on her especially because she was a child of 12 years old and wanted an adult she could trust and be supported by.

Lucy let herself get carried away by memories. The night had long fallen over the forest and the moon was watching over with its eye of light. She wished she could sleep without her nightmares, to be the happy child in a happy family agian. She knew she had to go back home to take her drug in order to resist the torture again.

Once she was in her room, Magi could not take her eyes off the mirrors. Whenever she moved, she could see her image and had the feeling of being watched. She had to do something about the mirrors. If she covered them maybe she could get rid of the feeling. She took two sheets from the drawer and covered them. She started to feel better, to move without being watched by her own person. Of course, it looked as if she was in a haunted room. She put on shorts and a T-shirt and went out into the corridor to head towards the bathroom.

The door of Fer's workshop suddenly opened and the impact between the two of them was so powerful that she slipped and would have hit her head against the wall if it weren't for an arm that stabilised her and she felt as all of her body collided against his. The emotion and surprise was so great that she could not get away from his embrace. A burning warmth captured her pelvis, oozing towards her toes, her heart pounding, her arms around his neck and under her lips, her artery throbbed as if all the blood gathered there. His breath burned her hair. Her sight blurred and she lifted her gaze towards him. She could not see his face but could feel his lips caressing her lips like a sigh and an electric discharge, like thunder gathered all the passion, the suppressed desires, forgotten emotions, all of them to create that magic moment. He detached himself, turned his back, and left her stuck against the wall wondering if it was only her fantasy. She remained in the same position to pull herself together and then entered the bathroom. She got stuck on the cold tile, she could see her troubled face, her legs were trembling and she could still feel the burn of thunder on her lips. Finally, she got in the shower and let the water run freely.

Fer started running towards the forest. He wanted to feel the cold air, to lie down on the wet ground to give it his suffering and all his desires. He was like a sleepwalker suddenly woken to reality, on the edge of the abyss, confused, not knowing where he was or where to go. Instinctively, he felt that anywhere he went meant his perish. He reached his hideaway, a small cave where he needed to crawl to enter and discover a room with a bed made of leaves and lichen, a stone table with a candle, and a few books. He always covered the entrance so that Lucy could not find it because she would never accept him to have a hidden place unknown to her. Had he not had that sanctuary, he was sure he would have killed himself a long time ago. He was so shocked that he experienced something so strange and lofty as he got lost in that woman that he was still feeling his body shivering. He lay down on the bed but the pain choked him, the discharge at touching her lips was so strong as though a red iron pierced him from head to toe. Lucy must have been afraid of this when she told him he was not allowed to touch women, only watch them. Was this the curse that mastered men taking away their will and leaving only desires?

Although it was the first time he touched a woman, he wanted her stuck on him, to caress her hair, lips, and eyes, to merge with debauchery, as Lucy said. He felt that if he wanted to keep her, he had to fight all the evil and fear planted in him by her, to fight all the drama of his family that he learned from his sister's stories that affected his childhood, adolescence, and maturity. He had always felt unfulfilled, something was missing, something that seemed to be where he was not allowed. At that moment, they were only one body as if they were born for each other. His fear disappeared, he was feeling strong, full of power, he felt the passion in her body and above all, he felt happiness. Could that be love? Could that be the love his sister had for him? No, it could not be the same love. Lucy loved him with a morbid love, she loved him with that hate that you can kill with, her love meant egoism, destruction, revenge. Having Magi in his arms, he felt non of that.. On the contrary, a joy invaded his soul, feeling it trembling inside, fragile and vulnerable but not for a moment did he think that it could hurt him. He wanted to protect her, to kiss her all over, to keep her there forever. Love can bring happiness or decay, that is what he understood at that moment. It was the first time he fell asleep with a smile on his face, with that small piece of happiness closed in his heart.

Once in her room, Lucy took her drug dose and opened the mirrors. At first, she did not realise what was happening, the image in the room was white. She thought it was the effect of the drug and opened the bathroom mirror too. At that moment, the door was opened with a jerk and a troubled Magi stumbled against the tiles. She was trembling and looked so transfigured, so lost... With eyes dripping venom, Lucy watched her and started thinking. What could make Magi look so passionate? Lucy was dumbfounded when a thought occurred to her. No, it could not be true, where could Magi have met Fer? How could such a close encounter happen to bring her to such a state? And Fer would never touch a woman that way, she scared him to death. And if it did happened, when and where? Lucy started going to and fro and when she looked in the mirror again, Magi was in the shower. Lucy waited for her to get out and watched her again, but this time calm and self- confident.

Maybe the drug was to be blamed. It seemed to her that lately her mind was playing tricks on her. Maybe she should be more careful with the dosage. No matter what it was, she would have to be very attentive in the future and watch them both. Why could she not see her room? Maybe she covered the mirrors. In fact, Magi had said that the mirrors were the only thing that troubled her and she could not understand the use of two big mirrors. Lucy replied that there was no place for them for the moment but she would find a solution. Tomorrow she would check if Lucy had covered them. No, she couldn't disturb Fer again, although she wished she could analyse him too as this would confirm that she hadn't lost her mind and if what she had seen was real. Lucy could wait, she had all the time in the world.

In her room, Magi lay down on the bed and thought about what had happened. How could such a thing happen? How could that man penetrate her so deeply as though he had been there all her life only in a few seconds? He was part of her soul and that moment put it in its place. Its place was there and she knew that nobody could take it away except in taking her life too. Why Fer, who was in fact, nobody but another woman's husband? What a strange couple, you never saw them together. They had separate bedrooms and what was more, on different floors. Why was everything so strange there? So may questions filled her head until she finally fell asleep.

THE DREAM

The force that entrapped her decided to defeat the obstacle. She was too weak to fight back and wanted to find out what was destined. It left her in front of the house on the lane, feeling in her thought:

– I can not help you any longer. You must go alone these few meters, cross the water, enter the yard and so you will hear and learn the magic spell "We the Great". Said the force and "danger, danger" was heard while disappearing into nothingness.

At the end of the fence, the sorcerer was waiting for her. Magi was not worried as she was at first, she was decided to go beyond the fence, over that stream. She did not understand who the sorcerer was or what "We the Great" meant. As if hearing her thoughts, a voice entered her mind and talked to her.

– This place is full of sickness, the Big Trouble. There is a magic cure called "We the Great" and your grandfather was the last sorcerer. He died before he could hand it over to your father. His soul is not accepted in the eternal life until he hands it over to one of the family members. He is before death and suffers tremendously. Without "We the Great", you can not defend yourself.

Magi watched him carefully and realized that the sorcerer in the lane was non other than her grandfather. He looked so old and thin, only his black eyes were burning behind the orbits. Suddenly he started trembling and vanished into the blue of the sky, whispering to her: You must hurry up, my time is up...

When Magi woke up, it was morning but she remembered the whole dream as if she had lived it. She could not believe she was in danger and then she remembered Fer and thought he might be. She would fall in love and Lucy would want to take revenge. She would have to avoid him, she was not going to start an affair with a man, especially a married one.

The morning passed with the usual chores, waiting for Lucy to appear and then going upstairs. Lucy looked so changed, like a ghost, her face so white like after a sleepless night, with a look of a sick person and a rictus in the corner of her mouth.

'I hope you are feeling fine?',
Mag asked Lucy worriedly.

'I feel as good as it gets.'
Lucy answered sharply and Magi dared not to ask anything more.

'You can go up to Fer's floor today because I do not know where he left.'

All day long Magi did the housework and after that, being satisfied with her work, she went to the terrace where she met Lucy who was enjoying a juice.

'I do not want to bother you but I would like to ask you something. I saw no telephone here and I would like so much to call my family and tell them I am ok.'

'But you told me you were not married.'

'It is true but my two sisters are waiting for my call and I do not want them to be worried.'

'Yes, we do not have a phone, the house is too far and the investment is expensive but we do not mind. When we go shopping, we visit our parents and children and we are better off without it. If one of your sisters speaks our language, give me the phone number and I will let her know you are ok.'

'Thanks a lot, they both speak the language but it is better to call the younger one, Juliet, so I will give you her number.'

'I can see you are excellent at doing the housework. I am pleased.'

'But it is not hard at all, that is why I would ask for permission to have a walk in the forest after I finish my work.'

'Sure, you may, but take care not to get lost.'

'Do not worry. My grandparents lived in the countryside and the forest and the mountains were close so I can find my direction.'

'Good night and do not fall asleep on the terrace because I will not be around to wake you up if you have a nightmare.'

'Thank you for your advice.'

Lucy kept asking herself where Fer had disappeared to. She suspected him of having a secret place but until now, she could not find it even though she followed him a few times. He would show up eventually because he would be hungry and had no clothes to change. She would have to go to the mine too and check on the victims. So far, she applied psychic torture which, in her opinion, was the most difficult to bear.

She entered a gallery, an ex-coal mine, that had a metal door with an inscription saying it was dangerous to enter. After unlocking the door, she lit a torch and continued to follow the road deeper into the mine. She reached another door that she unlocked and after a few meters, she stopped. She lit more torches around the place. She could use the lantern but the effect was not the same. She felt like she was in the heart of inquisition and she was the supreme judge. Carrying the torch, she reached a deep shaft, unlocked the lid, and looked inside. At the bottom there was a gutter full of living creatures like rats, cockroaches, earth worms... There was a small piece of ground, one meter high, and a bunch of rags on it. That was once a girl who came to work as a nanny for her. Now she was nothing but a shadow, a handful of bones crouched on a piece of ground. Once in a while, she used to throw her a bottle of water and some bread to keep her alive as long as she wanted. It was in her power to decide how long she would be alive for. She was amazed at her strength and decided to test her physical and psychic limits. Full of satisfaction, she closed the lid and went towards the cell to check on the other victim. This one had her legs and arms chained with the look of a chased animal. In each nanny, she could see her stepmother. She felt that her whole being revived from her suffering. They were the only ones whose suffering would stop with her. She asked herself many times if she stopped all this, if she stopped torturing her stepmother, would her pain stop too? Could she become a normal human being? She was convinced that even if she could stop herself, things had gotten too far and for too long. She left the mine, closed the doors, and went home. As long as she had them, Magi could wait.

Fer had not eaten anything for three days except forest fruits but he did not care. There was a stream too so he was not short of water. Oh yes, how much he missed her body warmth, lips, and hair smell, the arms around his neck, the heart vibration. He missed Magi.

That is why he was trying to stay as far as he could away until he was self-confident again. If his sister suspected anything he would be in great danger. He would have to wear the mask of carelessness and make her believe that he was the same. Lucy was like a predator, feeling any change and move and he was not convinced he could face her yet. He did not know and he did not want to know what had happened to that beautiful girl he had sympathy for. Lucy realised and reacted immediately. Then he disappeared from home for almost a week and when he came back, he thought she would cut him into pieces she was so mad. After spoiling him with her love, she said she had done everything for his own good, that if he had fallen into that witch's trap, it would have meant the end of their family. As if the two of them were a family. They were nothing but a couple of sick people, a weak man without any will and a woman sick of power and with an iron will. To hell with such a family! This time it was more than sympathy, it was the wish to have Magi next to him forever. That was why he could not risk anything, he had to pretend that he was the same weak man who was dominated by her.

For a few nights, the dream stopped haunting Magi. Maybe it was because of the long journey, the jet lag, and getting used to a new lifestyle. Maybe in her subconscious, she thought about the happiest period of her childhood together with her extraordinary grandparents. She was more pleased now that the ghost stopped appearing to her, which seemed to be of her grandfather. But something kept troubling her. Dreaming of your relatives and your childhood place meant something and was a warning for what was going to happen in the future, something terrifying meant something totally different. Her grandfather told her that she had a birthmark near her heart in the shape of a trefoil with four leaves which meant that she would have to pass over a great danger, like death, and it depended on her whether she succeeded to get over it. For this, she would have to know a few things that he could not tell her now because she was too young but the sign she was born under was very strong one and would protect her. Grandfather was a jack of all trades, he built houses, made furniture, shoed horses. Because he got married to Grandmother, whom he loved very much but she belonged to a poor family, he was disinherited. He used to bring Magi and her sisters sweets whenever he came back from work which Grandmother took quickly and hid, handing them out only in portions.

Grandmother was a very clever woman. She became a dressmaker in a nearby town, she learned to read and write by herself. All her seven children, who were still alive, were sent to school but with great sacrifices. "This is your only fortune" she used to tell them. That was why nothing seemed very hard to her. She worked from early morning till late at night to pay for her children's school. Despite all hardships, she had the heart of an angel. When she heard that somebody in the village needed a bed or a table, she gave hers to them as a gift and said "Your father will make another one, they need it more now." A long time after she had died, her memory was still very strong. Magi could see, feel, and hear their voices full of kindness, that of a noble soul. The time spent together with her grandparents was the fairy tale of her childhood. She knew that if she would spend more time in that magic place, she would fall asleep again so she stood up and left for her room.

Whenever Lucy paid visits to the mine, she seemed to be in a state of over-excitability, close to madness. She could see the agony of her stepmother, the wonder in those gray eyes, the horror, pain, and the begging. That moment was the beginning of her happiness, the happiness of revenge, the happiness of the suppressed. She wouldn't be able to stop seeking revenge and the more suffering she caused, the bigger her desire became to get revenge. Now she had the God's whip. Many times she thought of Him, implored Him to help her, to stop her suffering but she received no sign. Then she told herself there might be more than one God, both good and bad. Her God was probably the bad one, the merciless one. Maybe this was the sign she did not want to see, she had to strengthen herself, to endure, to gather the evil in her stepmother with the evil inside herself and hand it further. But she could not hand it over, she could hand it over only in the form of punishment. It was an amplified punishment because all the suffering stopped with him.

After marriage, her father used to go on business trips and was gone for days on end. Slowly and easily, her stepmother showed her true nature. She started to go away at night and even when her father was at home. Lucy heard his reproaches a few times but her stepmother used to embrace him, take him to bed, and prove to him that nothing he had imagined was true. She used to spend time with a girlfriend and he let her go out. He was understanding and he forgot all of a sudden.

More often, when he was away, her stepmother used to bring home dubious men, alcoholics, drug addicts and they threw parties until they collapsed. A few times, Lucy snuck out of her room and watched them. They were all naked, they poured whisky and champagne all over themselves, then started licking, touching themselves, no matter of sex, which led to perversities which they called erotic games. Her stepmother rarely brought the same persons twice, except a bald guy who was very thin like a skeleton with thick lips and bulging eyes. I did not understand what she could find in such a person until I felt it on my own skin. One evening, he found me hiding and told my stepmother.

'I can see something looking like a human being. I think you should give me that doll.'

Her stepmother watched her intensely and said:

'First I have to get her ready and later I shall hand her over to you, too. She needs her first lesson from her mother, that is how mothers do it. At least mine did it so.'

Lucy ran to her room, followed by their bursts of laughter. She locked her room, thinking about her helplessness.

Since that night, her stepmother was more cautious, at least when her father was at home. She was at home every night, she was extremely kind to them, Lucy and Fer. Her father was so in love that Lucy did not dare to say anything. She knew this was her stepmother's new scheme in case she would tell her father anything.

Lucy was 13 and she started to look good. She was tall for her age. Many times, she caught her stepmother watching her and analysing her with satisfaction. As if feeling something, she used to lock her room every night and be on the watch to hear the smallest noise. One night, when her father was not at home and there was a big noise downstairs, Lucy heard steps and laughter in front of her room. She knew who it was. Horrified, she hid in bed, pulling the blanket over herself. Seeing the closed door, her stepmother started to knock and call her name. Lucy covered her ears but when she pronounced the name of Fer, she ran to the door and asked her what she wanted.

'If you do not open the door, my little girl, I must go to your brother and I do not enjoy playing with somebody who does not resist.'

With trembling hands, Lucy opened the door and saw her stepmother almost naked with a bottle of drink in one hand and a cigarette in the corner of her mouth.

'That is how mum wants you, little tigress. Now, you cannot use your fangs and claws, it is time you felt mine. I have always wanted to stay with you in this pure bed. Be happy I did not give you over to that bald man yet, I shall teach you what my parents taught me, he will do the rest. This night I will make you feel only pleasure because without it, you will never reach the supreme pain.'

At that moment, Lucy's mind was blocked and in the morning when her stepmother left, she fell into a death-like sleep. She refused to understand what was happening to her, she protected her mind and so she was able to resist all those years. She was nothing but a puppy made of flesh and blood, used, thrown from one man to another until they got tired. She learned to be docile but, as if anticipating things, her stepmother used to say: "I know the tigress has claws but I would not like to feel them on my skin." Then she burst into laughter, letting the booze ooze on her neck, breasts, belly, and legs and made Lucy lick her saying she wanted herself washed properly so her father would not feel the smell. If she saw the least sign of disobedience in Lucy, she threatened to bring Fer down. Maddened by this idea, Lucy did whatever she was asked, even more. She started improvising lest she should get bored with her.

Those were the most important years of Lucy's life when she was supposed to have friends, to date boys, and feel the first thrill of love or despair, not hate and helplessness. Reaching her room, she seemed so weak that she hardly took the drug. She fell on the bed in her clothes and fell asleep.

One night, Fer snuck into the house to change his clothes and take some supplies. He knew Lucy used to take drugs to fall asleep so he was convinced she could not hear him. He was not ready yet to face her but he was more frightened to face Magi. How would he react? He was afraid he would not be able to control his body and mind and make a gesture that could betray him.

What if that evening meant nothing to Magi? What if she was a woman like any other for whom getting close to a man was nothing but an animal instinct ready to be broken loose? A normal attraction between them? He used to relive that moment a hundred times when he felt her vibrating, her hands around his neck, her lips, the electric shock, and the discharge when they touched one another. Maybe if he had not pulled himself away from her embrace and did not run like a coward, he would have understood much more. But he was so astonished, the warmth that seized him turned into a fire that seemed to burn him up and he knew that if he could not get out at that moment, he wouldn't show her the way anymore. And this would kill them both because at that moment, noone was ready to win. He would not have cared about death but she knew nothing of what was going to happen to her and it was not normal to endanger her. At the same time, he wanted to live but not like before. He wanted to live with her and feel her breath on his neck, to feel her pulsate within him, in his thoughts. Could it ever be possible? He wanted nothing except an ordinary life with that woman. He knew he was sick, his sickness was his past and present, it was not the creation of a sick mind.

Deep in his soul and body, he knew he was perfectly healthy. It was not a family legacy, it was the manipulation of shyness, fear, and lack of will. However, he did not feel like a weak man, he could tear himself away from Lucy. But living with her since he was little and indulging being pampered by her, he felt protected, and finally, he gave up. He was convinced that his sister protected him from lots of misfortunes. She sacrificed herself for him, and knowing how much he owed her, he let her run his life. He was aware of many things that had happened in the house, some of them he only guessed and others, not all, he found out from his sister. His relationship with his father was not so good. He was often away and when he came back, he used to have a few words with him and then he left again. After his marriage with the ex-nanny, on her persistent request, they moved to one of the houses that his father possessed, which was once a hotel at the foot of a mountain. It had two wings and his room was alone in one wing so he had a lot of space at his disposal. Lucy's room was not far from his but after an event that had happened one night, she moved close to their stepmother, telling him it was better for him and he should not be afraid because she would watch over him,. He was not afraid of loneliness. He had lots of computers and TV sets and a big library so he was pretty busy after school. Nanny used to bring the cleaning service especially when his father was going to come home.

In his kitchen, which was apart from theirs, he found absolutely everything, he lacked nothing. At school, all the pupils avoided him thinking he was the rich boy who could not be approached. That was ok for Fer because he was left alone. When his father died, he was found hanged, Fer passed pretty easily over it. Lucy seemed to have lost her mind. She had to be sent to hospital and kept sedated for a while because she wanted to take her life. It was a period when he truly felt free. His stepmother kept away from him. He knew she was angry with his father and if she could have, she would have killed him again. However, she left the house only after Lucy came home from the hospital. After a while, she disappeared altogether. He heard that she had left to an exotic country with the money left by his father.

Lucy was totally changed. Her look was haggard, wild, her nose seemed more pointed, her pretty mouth had a spasm at one corner and from time to time, she let out a sinister smile. She would wander from one room to another like a ghost in the middle of the night, talking to herself, threatening, swearing and many times crying. During day time, a nurse came to give her injections and pills. She told Fer to leave his sister alone for some time because she needed rest and not to worry because time would heal everything. His sister did indeed recover but not totally, and she did not depend on treatment any longer. She used to watch him, caress hime, and assure him that everything was going to be fine. After he had graduated from high school, she decided to sell the house and move there, a villa inherited from their mother's sister. She said she could not live in a crowded area and he accepted that, knowing how sick she was. Lucy opposed when he wanted to go to university and said she wanted him around at least for some time and suggested to attend long-distance courses. Fer was fond of history and his major was in medieval history, inquisition but he also started philosophy courses. Lucy helped him all the time. She got him rare books from auctions or old books stores and so she became an expert without a degree. Impressed by her knowledge and passion, he suggested she attend the same courses. She always refused and said she had everything she needed for what she was going to do. Many times he saw her tired, deep in thought, and sometimes her eyes expressed so much hatred that he was afraid to watch and most of the time, he stood aside.

Some nights Fer heard her screaming in her sleep, and after that talking to herself or leaving for the forest and coming back only at dawn. Fer was convinced she was sick again, that her life turned into tragedy after their father's death. He wanted to get rid of that place, of her, but whenever he tried to talk about it, she became depressed. From fury rages to heart-breaking begging and so he finally promised he would never part with her or at least as long as she lived. Now he realize he was caught in a spider web and the more he struggled, the tighter the web got around him but never close enough to affect his mind and maybe this was his salvation.

Still thinking about her grandparents, Magi went to her room. It was all quiet and she was happy because she did not want to meet any of them in such a state. After Fer's runaway, she did not know what to believe. She felt him avoiding her and it was not good. He might feel guilty for that strange kiss, for that moment of weakness and cheating on his wife. However, she intended not to repeat that experience or show him in words or gestures that she was affected by it. That brutal meeting was an accident, in fact, and so he had to see things too. It was nothing, a clash, a kiss and that was all. It was normal to feel excited because you did not collide with a piece of stone or a wall but a human being so she should not think about it any longer. She took a shower, went to bed, and started reading, falling asleep with the book on her chest.

The Dream

She was standing in front of the house and was watching the empty lane. Her feet were no longer stuck on the ground but she could not move. The wind was not blowing, the sun seemed stone-still in the sky as if the time had stopped. Nothing seemed to have life. "Maybe I arrived too late." She said to herself frightened, thinking that her grandfather might remain before death forever. She could not let him suffer so much. She felt like she had to help him get rid of that secret, that secret that kept him tied between the two worlds. She could see nothing but could feel the force that carried her up there. She felt it rising to the sun and then lowering towards her as if it came to life to be able to send the message.

The force was the connection between her and the sorcerer, it had to prepare her for the last meeting. When she would stand in front of the sorcerer, her mind and body would become one because only once with the sorcerer's last breath would he send the magic charm "We the Great" and she would have to memorise it from his last breath, only once. If she was not ready and could not memorise it, the sorcerer would be hanging between the two worlds forever and ever. When she woke up, it was 3 o'clock. Magi knew that she did not dream and that she was between the two worlds and her grandfather wanted to send her something, she would be ready to take over his burden and finally let him find his eternal peace. She had to believe that there was something bad in this place, something sick, something that needed the magic cure. She understood that the person who cooked that cure was willingly exposed to danger and could sacrifice her life in exchange for that person's recovery, offering the body and soul to God's disposal who, in his greatness, could change her into a messenger that would bring the cure. Now she understood why she had to be ready, she had to accept the danger that could mean death. To sacrifice yourself in order to save somebody's soul meant that you would have to be ready. She was not ready yet and her grandfather felt it, that was why he sent the force to teach her, to strengthen her, and see if she could accept the challenge. The force would be the one that decided the moment when the final encounter would take place. Magi felt more relieved now that she finally accepted everything that was happening to her, that somebody thousands of kilometers away from her country needed all the wisdom gathered by her ancestors and with that magic cure she could save a soul. This time she fell asleep but did not dream because peace had fallen in her soul.

In the morning, to her surprise, the three of them met for breakfast. It was the first time in the few weeks since her arrival, so she was excited and wanted everything to be perfect.

'Good morning, it is really a celebration for the three of us to be in the same place at the same time. It has not happened for a long time since the girl…'

Lucy's words stopped and she looked piercingly at Fer, as if she wanted to get into his soul.

'I am sorry to trouble you. I know you get up later and I only wanted a cup of coffee. I saw it was ready and I wanted to take advantage of the opportunity.'

He said hello with a total lack of interest and went up to his floor.

'Indeed, I apologised, I went upstairs sooner than usual.'

'Me, too, I could not sleep at all and I thought I could have my coffee sooner because I feel tired.'

They both had their coffee in silence and after that Lucy asked Magi.

'Would you like to go shopping with me today? We are going to a city 120 km away, we will buy everything we need and what you like and you can ring your sister up and towards the evening, we will come back.'

'Of course, I would like that but first I must finish my housework.'

'Forget about cleaning, it is not dirty anyway and then you can help me with my shopping, so it means you are working. Go and get ready, we are leaving in half an hour.'

She was so happy to finally get away from that hidden place that she flew up the stairs and was ready in 15 minutes. Any trace of suspicion disappeared. What could be wrong with this? They would have a walk in the city, do the shopping she would call up her family. She thought everything was in her imagination, she was too tensed up. Everything seemed abnormal with this family and indeed the relationship between the two of them did not seem too affectionate but that happened in so many families, she was not there to judge anybody. So she forgot about her grandfather that was the sorcerer and about the Force and about "We the Great." There was nothing except the joy of going shopping. Lucy appeared in 20 minutes completely changed. She was dressed in sportswear with the best quality clothes. She had her hair arranged and the reddish locks were falling disorderly, throwing sun sparks. Her lips had pink lipstick and her make-up made her look 10 years younger. Magi could not hide her surprise.

'Lucy, you look great, you are really beautiful. I think many men will admire you today!'

Then she realised her blunder because she was a married woman. To her surprise, she laughed.

'I did not think about it, not for a minute but I am glad you reminded me of other men except Fer. Not that I am tempted but it is good to still be admired, it is good for the ego.'

Magi was wearing a pair of new blue jeans bought second hand, a T-shirt without sleeves and some Chinese sports shoes that were in fashion. She did not look bad but compared to Lucy she seemed like the poor relative. Luckily Magi was not bothered because she came to make money and not to conquer somebody. Lucy took out a big car that she called the truck and off they went. Lucy was in high spirits so they chatted all the time. Lucy asked Magi about her family, about her future plans. Time passed quickly and they reached the little town where they had to do the shopping. They first stopped at a supermarket as big as a warehouse. Lucy filled the car with food enough for one season and bought absolutely everything they wanted. When they finished, it was afternoon so Magi decided to phone home. They stopped at a telephone booth where Lucy dialed the number several times and finally heard her sister's voice. It was night in her country but of course, she did not mind. On the contrary, she was glad because the whole family was worried by Magi's silence. She explained everything, promising that Lucy or her would call again.

'Now that you calmed down your family and we finished shopping, what about an ice cream?'

'Of course, I like ice cream very much, especially caramel.'

After they had eaten a delicious ice cream, they got in the car and left home. It was already evening and when they arrived, night had fallen. Magi took all the shopping out of the car, took it into the house and tired but satisfied with the day, she went directly to the shower. Under the shower stream, she thought there was no better place than this one, that she started to feel more and more comfortable with this strange family. Magi jumped into bed and fell asleep without thinking of anything.

The Dream

Magi was standing at her place in front of the house and was waiting. She felt a breeze coming from above. It was the Force but she sensed it was weak and sad, hardly having the power to whisper.

'You are dominated by the evil…'

'What have I done? Where is your power?'

'My power resides in you, my force lies in your force. When you are weak in front of danger, you make me weak too. When you see nothing because of the spell, you can lead us to destruction. Wake up until you can be woken up. Do not forget that the sorcerer is waiting for the last Eucharist. If you get lost, "We the Great" will disappear and your grandfather will live forever in the eternity of pain.'

Then it vanished and Magi remained in the middle of the country road feeling very sad. When she woke up her soul was so heavy, she felt so weak and sad, she could not understand where she went wrong. Her sleep was so agitated for the rest of the night and she woke up deep in thoughts and powerless.

Lucy was happy to have won Magi's trust with a walk, a phone call home, and a lot of chat. How easy everything was. At the beginning, Lucy thought Magi would be more suspicious. Lucy thought she was more profound, especially because she asked questions that disturbed her. As for Magi's family, it was easier than lucy had expected. Magi had told them that either Lucy or Magi would call. The roars of laughter started like artillery. That was why Lucy preferred girls from forgotten countries, they were easier to manipulate, naïve, and credulous and their trace was easy to be erased.

From time to time, they sent money, their families were pleased and the rest did not matter. The last time Lucy visited her victims, they were still alive. She threw them bread and water and left them in their agony. She was in good shape and she could face another night of memories.

They were all downstairs, on the ground floor, surrounded by the friends of Lucy's stepmother. They were all drunk, drugged and she was the leader. It was then that she heard her life story. It was years since her first night, years that she succeeded to hide everything from her father. He thought that finally, they had made peace and this made him extremely happy, especially when he heard his wife say.

'How could I not love her? She is my dearest little girl, she satisfies all my wishes the way I do when it's my turn.'

She used to laugh as she watched Lucy in a way only she was able to understand. So her father left satisfied with his unified and harmonious family. When Lucy's stepmother was on drugs, she felt the need to tell the story of her family. Lucy heard that she had been abused physically and mentally by her both parents, that they were on drugs, and when they had no money for drugs, they used to rent her to their friends. Before Lucy's stepmother was 16, she ran away from home and since then she knew nothing about them and she was not even interested in them. Of course, she thought about showing up at their door in the latest car design and full of money, to make them kneel in front of her and eventually to shoot one bullet in their heads but she said it was not worth it. And then Lucy thought that if she had disappeared, nobody would look for her, nobody would ask about her. Since that moment, Lucy started concocting different plans to get rid of her stepmother but she realized the right time had not arrived yet. The fact that she could think of her extermination made her resist.

Fer saw Magi and Lucy leaving together and understood that Lucy had changed her tactics. She probably felt Magi did not trust her completely and maybe a car ride, going shopping, and having a chit-chat would get the two women closer. Finally, he should find a way to meet Magi without Lucy's knowledge and warn her. He did not think about how to do this without telling her the whole truth, that they were brother and sister. If he told her that she would think him mad or worse, she would think he wanted to take advantage of her, especially after what had happened in the basement. He knew it would be hard to convince her, no matter the means he used. He caught Lucy entering the deserted mine many times but he never had the courage to go there. He was suspicious and this was frightening him to death. He thought that the next time that Lucy was missing, he would go and search the mine because he was very curious and the desire to find the truth had been torturing him for a while. He did not have the curiosity to open the mirror to watch Magi. He found out from his sister that Magi had covered the mirrors in the room and it made him happy. Magi did not spend too much time in the shower which deprived Lucy of having great pleasure. Hence the change in tactics that occurred lately, to win Magi's confidence.

The questions related to the children and to the phone made Magi stay alert. Fer was sure Magi asked herself about Fer and Lucy's relationship but not aloud and Lucy guessed it. Now Lucy was trying to convince Magi that their family was a little strange and she was sacrificing herself for Fer's sake, like any wonderful wife. If the two women started to get on well together, it meant it would be hard for him to make Magi believe him. It would be an unequal battle but Fer had the upper hand – Lucy thought she knew him but he was sure he knew her better. All day long he had been thinking of the situation to find a credible way to approach Magi. Finally, he realized he did not have the slightest idea so he left everything to chance. The simplest solution was the one you could not see because you could not believe it was so simple. When he saw them coming back, he realised Lucy had made progress but it was only the beginning and there was still hope. The most important thing was that Lucy would not persist in her tactics. He knew she didn't have much patience, she was too confident in her power to manipulate. She thought she knew and understood everything. But even the most feared pray animal endowed with the sharpest senses became pray in the end because of too much confidence. He wanted her to not come to his room tonight and to see her triumph, her grin full of malicious satisfaction and her sick desire to see him subjected, to feel him dependent on her. To his great joy, she went directly to her room, probably satisfied with the day and confident in her plans, as usual.

During the next weeks, the two women had coffee together more often. Lucy was trying to gain Magi's confidence and that was why she was making the effort of being around Magi more often, to advise her like an older sister taking you under her protective wing. Magi did not like this new turn of events, she felt the effort, everything sounded wrong, nothing was coming from the heart. Magi had the sixth sense that made her keep her distance, she did not trust people before she did not know them better and this family was keeping her with tense. Magi did not show it to Lucy, on the contrary, she let her believe she had won her friendship and seemed subjected to any of her advice.

That night, after she had finished all her duties, she felt the need to take a walk through the forest, it was like a call that was coming from everywhere. She followed the first lane she could see. It was as if something was attracting her and as though pushed by a force, she went deeper and deeper into the forest. Suddenly she woke up as if from a dream. She looked around and realized she was in the forest of her childhood. There was the old oak under which she slept so many times while her grandfather told her stories and the river that was singing a lullaby. She was tired so she lay down under the oak and fell asleep.

THE DREAM

Magi was standing upright in front of the fence. There were only a few meters between her and the fence. Suddenly, a strong blow in her back made her stagger and she was ready to fall but she caught herself quickly, watching all around her. She could see nothing but was sensing a presence around her. Then a second blow that could not move her. The blows succeeded one after the other, so powerful that she could hardly breathe and keep her balance. She did not expect it, she could not understand what kind of a game it was, and if it did not stop she would lose her balance and fall in the dust of the lane. She was determined to resist as much as possible. She heard a strong roaring from above and saw a twister threateningly falling down upon her as if wanting to suck her in. It enveloped her with the force of a hurricane, staggeringly going around her, swinging her to and fro but it did not succeed to detach her. Then suddenly, it was all quiet and peace fell down over her. She felt the force squeezing her mind, whispering:

'Your forces have grown from one day to another and they will become even stronger so that when the Healer sends you the magic charm, you will be ready. This can be heard only beyond the gate, when you step over you will hear it and learn it. "We the Great" is a magic and complex cure. The chosen one "The Sorcerer", starts at dawn on an initiated journey that he takes into the seen and unseen world, in the heart of the elements he gathers, water, ants, earth, tree twigs, stones. You need 9 big wooden spoons, a big clay pot with a circle or a wooden pail, and a copper knife. If you lose one spoon the man for whom you want to break the charm dies.' Strengthen your spirit and body for the chosen moment …

Magi was startled. She rubbed her eyes unaware of her whereabouts. Everything unrolled in front of her eyes and she knew she was directed towards that place because only "a man could enter a new world, the world of the beginnings, containing all the gifts and powers for renewing life because life is born every day." It was as if the innocence of her childhood was blending with the power of maturity in order to defeat the evil. Now she felt ready to confront something or somebody existing in that place. She watched the old oak once again, she saw her grandfather stroking her hair while she was falling asleep.

Magi knew she would never find this place again, that her grandfather had opened himself like a gate towards the other world so that she could understand and believe that something that she would soon be confronting was happening here. She started to go home sad and happy, worried, but with a new force she felt inside her.

Lucy was feeling more and more distressed. She was wandering in the forest, talking to herself and her father, but she was haunted most by the image of her stepmother. Even now, she could see those eyes filled with horror and amazement when she found herself buried up to her neck with legs and arms tied up. She could not believe that she, the mistress of all evil, who had conducted everybody in this house, let herself be tricked by a teenage girl. If she could have killed Lucy with her eyes at that moment, Lucy would be dead now. Next to her lay the dead body of the bald man, having his extra big penis cut, with a grin of pain around his lips. It was only then that she understood the whole atrocity, she found herself standing in front of the supreme judge, in front of her own creation, that there was no mercy and her death would be a agony.

She could not speak but even if she could have, she had nothing to say. What she created was right there in front of her and the cruelty and satisfaction on the face of her creation said everything.

Not even now could she understand why she remained in the house after her father's suicide, maybe it was fate. The truth was that Lucy stayed in the hospital for one year, that was so sick she was and she imagined that she would be declared mad and that her stepmother would manipulate Fer. Her father started to realise that something was happening. Although she tried to cover up everything, her stepmother was so sure of herself that she did not care whether her father was at home or not, she used to bring her friends, throw decent parties when he was present, and when the rows started to be violent, she reproached him for staying alone too much, that she needed fun, friends. Lucy's father started to check the bills for food, drinks, cleaning, and more things the house did not need. He tried several times to ask me but it was already too late, I trusted nobody, especially him. I knew he would abandon us at her smallest sign of tenderness. I told him only this: "I am sorry for everybody but it is too late." The memories made her tired. Every time she took a soul, she took a part from her life, too. Each death was her death until nothing would be left. She did not feel the same satisfaction as she did at first, she could see in each nanny the face of her stepmother and sometimes she almost pitied them. The kind nature she had in her childhood would pierce through the tough shell and shake her wish of revenge. She feared this most. Her senses started to grow older if she could relive that happy period of her childhood. However, it was too late for her, she did not choose her destiny. Most of the time she blamed her father for everything and the fact that he committed suicide proved that she was right. He did not have the courage to face the situation. He chose the most convenient solution for himself, he abandoned them again and this was too much for her to bear. She felt true loneliness, she knew that, in fact, she was protecting him because her stepmother was never interested in Fer. He was the weak one who lacked will. She sacrificed her childhood for the family she thought was united and happy. Her father let her face everything alone and so that, in his selfishness, he could be happy. Maybe he felt that something was happening in the house but it did not change anything about his sick love for her stepmother. Or maybe he had to give them up, it would have made him feel guilty for the memory of their mother, so he refused to see the truth sacrificing her for his weakness. When Lucy realised she had been used by her father too, she wanted to commit suicide. She lost her mind, betrayed by the most important man in her life.

She hardly recovered, tried to accept the situation but resignation was replaced by revenge. Had she not found her step mother in the house when she came back from the hospital, had she left immediately after her arrival when she was still living between fiction and reality, maybe she would have tried to forget and find a way to go on with her life. But she was there, spying on her, watching the progress or regress of her disease, analysing her.

Maybe her stepmother was convinced that she could still dominate her and keep her on a leash like a faithful dog. She believed that debauchery entered her so deeply that she could not give up and she would remain the conductor of the orchestra. What her stepmother did not know was that after each party she was obliged to attend, she went up to her room and played out different scenarios of revenge and that helped her not to crack. In fact, killing her stepmother was revenge on Lucy's father, he had to die as many times as she died. She had to draw a conclusion in one way or another, to put an end to the hateful revenge but the last step was her encounter with her father. She knew she was before death, her time was up, but she was not worried. On the contrary, she was happy with fulfillment. She had no time because the countdown had started. Not even the drug could ease her suffering or the long walks until morning. Her mind could not face so many memories, her body was ground inside by the disease of soul and drugs. She had to find the solution for the road to hell, the last stepmother that would perish to define her creation. The last punishment would be her first start, it would help her take the image of the beginning, she would throw away all the others from her mind, only one remaining – her stepmother.

Fer became more and more worried. He saw Lucy agitated, her eyes playing in orbit seemed blurred, and her look got through him without seeing him. She was rambling and running aimlessly as if she wanted to find something. A few times, he heard her talking to their father, warning him, begging him, and then bursting into a heart-breaking cry. He wanted to approach her, to caress her and embrace her, he knew she was sicker than before. Her voice was changed as if the little girl from childhood was running happily to jump into daddy's arms. She preferred their father and he had always liked her more. Then her voice became furious, more mature, fighting with herself, with their father, with their stepmother, with the whole universe, cursing their father for leaving them alone. She cursed Fer for being so helpless – at that time they had different names which they later changed.

Sometimes her voice was that of their stepmother's, mewing like a cat in a rut or laughing in morbid, vulgar roars. Maybe she should be sent to hospital again but how could he do that without her feeling that somebody was approaching the house? She could kill them all if she suspected anything. He would have to go by night almost 100km to the nearest town and explain to the authorities who they were and all that was happening.

But they would not believe him because Lucy was on good terms with the most important people there, donating money for charitable actions. Everybody had an excellent opinion of her but not of him. She had explained to them that they chose to live so isolated because of Fer, that the noise and crowd made him furious, and sometimes it was hard to control him. And there were the two girls that he had found in the mine shaft. He needed an extraordinary power to sneak to the mine. After he visited Lucy one night and saw her so drugged that she would sleep all night long. But the door was locked so he had to come back to her room and find the keys. Lucy was sleeping with her clothes on, thrown across the bed as if the sleep had caught her so quickly that she fell as she was, only her eyes were running behind the lids as if followed by a demon. When she changed her position and started mumbling, Fer was sure she would wake up and catch him there. However he was self-controlled and would have told her that she was screaming so loud that he had decided to go downstairs and see if he could help her. Fer easily found the keys because there were 3 in one bunch. He supposed it was the right one, grabbed them and ran to the mine. Holding a flashlight, he opened the door. He saw the second door and entered into what looked like a cell. When he lit it, he burst into a yell of horror. He dropped the flashlight and his first impulse was to run away. He seemed to have arrived in a different time. One figure that seemed to have been a woman chained was leaning against the wall. He was sure she was dead but when the flashlight lit her face, her eyes deep in orbit moved and it was then that he saw death. A few rags were hanging on her body, the wounds were suppurating, others were bleeding, the shit mixed with urine turned his stomach upside down. He approached her but she did not move, she was a living dead. He turned her face towards him and started to talk to her. He did not know if she understood anything but he could see a glitter in her eyes and her head seemed to move a little. He told her to hang on, that he would do anything to save her. He did not know when but he would come back with some food. He caressed her and even kissed her on the forehead.

When Fer was ready to leave, he saw an iron lid. Although it was late and he was scared that Lucy might wake up, he guessed that the last key belonged to it so he unlocked it. He was tougher than before but he started to cry, he yelled, he wished he could have died. On the bottom of a shaft that stank like a rotten corpse, on a small piece of land that protruded from the gutter, there was something deformed, like a pack of rotten rags forgotten there for ages.

Whatever or whoever it was, it was impossible to be alive, nothing was moving. When he lit the place up he saw a bottle with a little bit of water in it and more empty bottles lying around. He supposed those rags had drunk the water not long ago so perhaps she was still alive. He started to shout, to talk to her, to encourage her the same way he did with the other one. She was either dead or she believed nothing but she did not move at all.

It was too late for him to stay so he hurried to wipe his traces, to lock up everything, and run towards the house praying that Lucy had not woken up yet.

It was almost daylight, the house was deep in silence. When Fer arrived in front of the door, he heard the shower but he had to leave the keys so he opened the door slowly and snuck inside. He managed to put them in their place and the moment he shut the door, she came out of the shower. He got stuck behind the door fearing to move and give himself away. He heard her approaching and snarling as if she sensed something. She hesitated a while, then she headed towards the table, took the hairdryer, and started to dry her hair. It was then that he had the power to fly to his room. He blamed himself for not having the courage to go to the mine so far. In fact, he should have felt something, especially after the disappearance of that pretty girl. In his subconscious, he knew it but he refused to see the truth. He was exactly like his father, afraid that his imaginary world would fall apart, sacrificing his children and Fer sacrificed some lives that had nothing to do with Lucy's tragedy and now the same fate was waiting for Magi. The girls were the emergency now, all he could do now was give them food, water, and some medicine to keep them alive until he found the rescuing solution. He would talk to Magi and ask her to cook something and tell her how tasty her native country's food was. Then he would go to the girls more often to feed them and encourage them. He would have to warn Magi too, maybe he would show her the mine and explain everything.

Magi woke up with the first sun rays but she could not get out of bed. She was reliving the dream she had had that night. She knew it was not only a simple dream but the last stage of preparation. In fact, she felt so strong confronting the force that she felt she could move the mountains.

'This is the last time we shall meet. From now on you are the force, I was the sign of destiny gathered in eternity to guide you towards your fate. "We the Great" is a powerful cure and it is accompanied by a magic charm that is powerless without it. I will tell you what you have to do but you must learn the magic charm from the Sorcerer. If you do not learn it all at once, it will get lost forever and the Healer will not be accepted by the earth.'

The Sorcerer will leave his house at dawn, freshly washed, having not eaten yet and having not talked to anyone, armed with 9 great wooden spoons, a copper knife, and a big clay pot with a circle. He will practice the black fast, the fast of silence, and will be praying all the way. Wandering through the fields and the forest, until he finds 9 waters that he will take with the 9 spoons each, 9 spoons of water, asking the vital liquid for help. Then he will take one ant from the 9 ant hills and clay from 9 ant hills without ants. He will take 9 tree twigs from 9 different trees, asking for forgiveness to each one for the wound he causes: " I did not come to harm you, I came to get power and health..." He will place a little stone found in the 9 waters in the pot. He will cut the twigs with the copper knife so it does not get oxidised and place them in the water pot. By the end of the day when it gets to the sick man, a part of the twig's juice will have mixed with the water, forming a mixture. The Sorcerer will be free of fast only after the sick person is sprinkled and the charm is pronounced and the sick person drinks from the mixture. Gathering "We the Great", the Sorcerer will make a new world, counting the elements from nine to one, from this present to the beginnings, turning all the evil caused by sickness to the moment 0, when it did not exist. The pot in the hand of the Sorcerer is a small terrestrial globe, a pure physical world, clean and perfect, where there is no sickness, desperation, or death. He must get self-integrated into the elements because he is the Great Creator, capable of passing through the soul and body, suffering the disease of the person he set off for.

It was then that Magi felt it for the last time, how it scattered as the stars rained into nothingness. She had everything in my mind, not even a breath was forgotten, it was as if she was reading a book.

Lately, she saw Lucy so changed and distant, as if she was avoiding her. It did not bother her too much but she thought she might have done something wrong. For a few times, she heard her talking to somebody but when she got closer, there was nobody except her. If she could meet Fer, maybe she could understand what was happening to Lucy but he was not to be found as if he had disappeared. Reading her mind, probably, Fer came downstairs.

'Hello, Magi, I hear you are doing just fine. My wife is extremely pleased with you.'

'Hello, I am glad to meet you because I wanted to ask about her. Is she sick because she is avoiding me?'

'She is sick, indeed, and in this state, she hates talking to anybody. The best way is to leave her alone. It is only a nervous breakdown and I hope she will recover. By the way, I would like to ask you something... Would you mind cooking something from your native country? With lots of meat and vegetables and if it is not too much, I would like a cake, too. If Lucy asks anything, do not tell her it is for me because I know she will get upset and I do not want to add to her distress. Tell her simply that you miss cooked food. And something more, if you notice the food is missing, do not panic. I will let you know when I need more. Thanks and do not give me away.'

Magi remained watching him while he walked away. All she understood was that he wanted her to cook for him and Lucy should not find out. What could be so bad in it? She would do what he has asked her to do.

Fer seemed changed too, he did not seem the man Lucy had described to her as weak and sick. He did not look sick at all. He did not seem the type of man who preferred loneliness, who was retired and shy. On the contrary, the roles must have changed.

After she had finished cleaning up, she started cooking. She chose a chicken and cooked some stew with all the vegetables on earth, then she baked a very appetising raisin cake. Happy to have finished her work, she retired to her room after a good shower. She did not see Lucy at all, it seemed she had retired to her room earlier. Because she could not sleep, Magi thought of climbing the roof. She had longed to do this but until now she was not ready.

She climbed the window and with a little effort, she reached the ladder and climbed to the top. Luckily the opening in the glass roof was big enough and she could squeeze through. She was a good climber and was not afraid of heights. In her childhood, she used to sit on the roof of the house or on tree tops and her grandmother used to scold her out of fear of her falling down. She started to explore the roof from all angles to see which place was the most comfortable and where she could get the most beautiful view. Suddenly, she stopped and stared down startled. She was exactly above Fer's terrace. Luckily he was not there otherwise he might have thought she was spying on him. Hearing noises in the garden, she stood still not to give herself away. She saw Fer heading towards the forest and carrying a ladder. After a while, he reappeared, entered the house and Magi decided it was time to return from the terrace, to get nearer to the place she had climbed up. After a while, Fer appeared again, this time carrying a pretty big backpack and following the same route, getting lost in the forest. Magi was really amazed. What could he be doing in the middle of the night and what were those things for? She went back to her room trying not to think of those things anymore.

Lucy knew she had reached the limit and if she wanted to reach the end as she had planned, she needed a lot of rest. It was easy to say, hard to do. In order to succeed she would have to increase her drug dose and it was exactly now that she should be watching the two of themcarefully. But her body gave up and so she had no other option. She did not suspect anything about Fer and Magi. She was relieved about it so she could have a little rest. She took a bigger dose and felt she was falling asleep before getting to bed.

She saw the door opening and her father entering without being announced. Her stepmother and the others were in the middle of terrible debauchery. Her stepmother came with dozens of guys again. It was her birthday, she was 33 and she said she was going to have a hell of a party because her father was expected back only in 2 days. She pretended to ask him to come back earlier for her birthday but he said it was a business too important to be postponed. But he promised to make her an unforgettable surprise. He even called her that evening to tell her how much he loved her and asked her not to be sad because he was not there physically, only with his soul, promising to make it up to her. She hung up laughing and started to mock him in front of those scumbags gathered from bars. Lucy's heart was weeping and she had to take part in that masquerade.

When the door opened, her father caught them in the middle of the most perverse sexual games that Lucy took part in too. Her father had come with lots of gifts, lots of cars because he could not carry everything alone. He had 33 baskets with 33 flowers, each being amazingly beautiful, 33 different brands of champagne, huge plates with caviar, and other goodies. A car, specially designed for her was waiting in front of the villa. He turned back, shut the door, brought everything on the front terrace, and left. At first, nobody moved, nobody could say a word despite the drinks and drugs inside everyone. Hearing the cars leaving, her stepmother rushed outside but it was too late, her father had left. Without any remorse, she made everyone carry the things inside, saying she had plenty of time to make up with the old man but today it was her birthday and nobody would ruin it, not even an old and impotent husband.

Lucy saw her father only when he was found hanged a week later. He had his will changed and had left everything to Lucy and Fer but he loved her stepmother so much that he had left her

5 million dollars. At first, she was so angry that she threatened to take them to court but in case of adultery, she received nothing, as was specified in the prenuptial contract. The people who accompanied her father that night were witnesses and she realised she could lose everything so she finally resigned. But Lucy did not and when she came back from the hospital and she no longer depended on the medication, she prepared her revenge. The only friend her stepmother still brought home was the bald man who caused Lucy so much pain together with her stepmother. Lucy had chosen an isolated place in advance and she paid some workers to dig two big graves. One evening when they were on drugs as usual, she poured sleeping pills in their drinks. The rest was easy, she carried them to the car and took them to the prepared place. She buried her steppmother up to her neck, she cut off his penis and threw it into his mouth. She was sorry he could not wake up because of all the drugs and drinks, so he died in his sleep. But she kept her stepmother alive until she got sick of her face. But she did something good, she donated the 5 million dollars to a foundation for abused children called "And tomorrow" and after that, she disappeared as if she had never existed. She did not sell the house as she ahd told Fer. She found an explanation to move out saying it was the best solution for her to recover.

Towards evening, Fer tried to contact Lucy but she rejected him and said she was too tired and she wanted to have a rest. He had not heard her say "I want to rest, let us postpone it for some other time" in a long time. In fact, there was nothing he had to talk to her about, he just wanted to check on her and see if he could take the keys of the mine that night. He was very worried about the girls' condition. He hoped to find them alive, at least one of them, and he knew he had to hurry up if he wanted to give them the slightest chance. Lucy paid him no more visits so he was relieved. When all the noises had stopped, he started to carry the things he needed to the mine. The ladder to go down the shaft, the medicines, the food cooked by Magi, and a lot of water. He made the bottles look exactly like his sister's bottles because he could afford no mistake. This was the first priority for the time being. When all the things were taken to the chosen spot, he went back home and waited for the moment to sneak inside and take the keys. It was late at night when he opened the door and entered. Lucy was sleeping as if she was dead. At first, he thought she might have been but the soft breathing that was heard through her opened lips showed she was alive, as if she was in a coma. He took the keys, snuck out, and rushed to the mine. He carried everything inside the inquisition room, as Lucy called it. When he approached the girl in chains and lifted her head, he realised she had recognised him. He could hardly feed her, thanking Magi for the nourishing food. At first, she refused the food, her mouth was clenched, she was staring and he was afraid she might go into shock. He started to talk to her kindly and explain to her why he was there and what he wanted to do. Later, she watched him as if she wanted to talk to him and he knew that he had made the first step towards her mind. She started to eat while he explained his plan. He asked her not to give up, even if she would not see him for a few days, as it meant he could not come but he was around. He cleaned her wounds, disinfected them, and used some antibiotics. That was all he could do for the time being and he told her she should not show any sign of recovery when Lucy appeared. The hours passed quickly and he had to check the shaft. He opened the lid, put the ladder in and descended. Nothing was moving except some rats but the death smell that was all around made you think you were in hell. He approached the mass of bones that was crouched on the ground.

He felt a gust of fresh air and watching closer, he noticed an opening in the wall and realised it was an old vent. Luckily he had put on his rubber boots, otherwise he would have been in mud up to his knees. At first, he wanted to give up thinking he was too late. Then he saw her chest bones moving slowly and touched that living skeleton, talking to her. Having survived under those conditions was due to a strong will and that thin fresh air. Her bones were deformed because of the position she was always sitting in, so he crouched next to her trying to establish contact and make her understand that he came to help. If she thought he was Lucy's husband, she might believe that they were in this macabre thing together so the most important thing was to gain her trust step by step. Explaining to her that he had known nothing of her situation, he felt a little relaxation while he was caressing her back bones. Fer told her exactly what he had told the girl above, he asked her to help him feed her, to let him see her wounds because time was very precious now. He barely succeeded in putting her in an upright position but she could not stand on her own so he leaned her against the wall. When she opened her mouth and started eating as greedy as a wild beast, he saw she had lost most of her teeth. He asked her to chew longer before swallowing, to help her stomach digest. Noticing a recess in the wall, he left a great portion of the food there. The bottles with water were not a problem as they got lost amongst the others. Her eyes were so thankful that he wanted to hold her in his arms but he was afraid that what was left of her could break in his hands. He was impressed by the way she managed to survive. The empty bottles of water were arranged like a bed next to the vent, protecting her from the dampness of the ground. She would not have resisted longer but he was sure she would have struggled up to the end. He assured them he was going to do everything he could to come as soon as he could and find a way to save them. He knew they were both determined to fight so he gained their trust and his first mission in this world was to "never abandon hope." For the first time, he felt strong, he was convinced that if the dragon of the story appeared now he would be the winner. He hurried to erase any trace of him being there, to lock up everything and hide the ladder, to reach the house, and put the keys in their place. He was so happy that his first mission ended without any incident but he did not want to sit on his laurels because the real trial was coming soon. Tired but content at the same time, he fell asleep but his mind was making plans for the future.

Magi woke up in the morning and thought about what she had seen the night before. What could Fer use the ladder for and what was he carrying in the backpack? She knew she could not ask him but this did not make her less curious. She started working in the kitchen, waiting for Lucy and Fer upstairs to wake up so she could go there to tidy up. All of a sudden, she felt a hand grabbing her.

'Thanks for the food.'

He whispered, putting a finger on his lips like an accomplice and continued.

'It is our secret. If everything goes well and we are not suspected, soon I will ask you to do something more but I prefer a very consistent meat soup. Do not ask me any questions, all in good time.'

Hearing a noise from upstairs, he quickly left.

Lucy seemed more refreshed and in a better mood than before.

'Hello Magi, I noticed you are the first in the kitchen. Have you had your coffee already? If yes, no problem, I will have it alone.'

'Hello, I am glad you feel better, I was worried about you but now I can see everything is OK. I had my coffee and I was waiting for you to get up so I can go upstairs. If you want me to keep you company, I will do it most gladly.'

'Thanks for your concern but I prefer being alone for some time. I have not been feeling well lately but a few days of rest will get me back to my feet. I think you can go upstairs to Fer too, as far as I know, he is not there.'

Lucy had a pretty good night and it was because she took a bigger drug dose. It was not the first time she did it and it worried her a little but she knew she had no choice. She took her coffee and went to the wonder terrace where she could feel the spirit of her mother. It was the house that they inherited from their aunt and the terrace witnessed many happy moments in the life of the two sisters. Their parents used to sit there for a chit-chat with friends till late at night. It was there that they played princesses and it was there where she met Lucy's father for the first time and they swore to each other eternal love. It was really a magical place as if taken from a fairy tale, a place of good things.

Lucy wanted to keep it a secret, to enclose it under a dome but the terrace was living and blooming from nature, it was a part of it. She could see herself young, beautiful, surrounded by friends, and imagining one of them being her life partner. She was surrounded by the love and beauty of the human spirit here, by beginnings without pain, here the world was spinning around her. That was why she avoided spending too much time here because her spirit became weak, she let herself be overcome by love, she was sick with despair and indulged herself into a sweet and serene peace of mind.

Magi went to the second floor to start her routine work. She was in a hurry to finish it before Fer arrived. When she entered the small kitchen, she saw the empty pot and she wondered how he could have eaten everything in such a short time. Later, she remembered the night she had seen him carrying some things and that explained it. Maybe he had found a poor family and wanted to help them, knowing that maybe Lucy would not agree. This thought made her happy because for a while she had a hard time too and she had nothing to eat. Helping some poor people meant he had a good heart and he was a special man. She felt attracted to him, both physically and mentally, as if a magnet was between them. She avoided being next to him because she always had butterflies in her stomach and an avalanche of feelings might start. The kind that you look for your whole life to be a complete person. She could not understand how a sick person could be so healthy. She went to the first floor and started with Lucy's room, as usual. It was the first time she saw a syringe on the night table. She smelled it and a pungent smell penetrated her nose and she shook disgustedly. God! What kind of medicine could that be? Was she so sick that she injected herself? She realized she had not seen any kind of medicine in Fer's room, although she was told he was the sick one. She had often seen a ring with 3 keys on it, reminding her of old-time prisons, but it was probably the passion for the old things she had seen all over the house. She placed everything back and continued her work.

Later in the evening, Magi took a walk in the forest feeling fresh and full of life. She could hear the sleeping pulse of the earth, the serenity of the night full of rustling leaves, and her desire to have Fer by her side. Having him on her mind, she went back to her room.

She could not sleep so she decided to climb up to the roof again. Once she was up, she headed towards the place where she could see his terrace. Without thinking, she leaned forward to see better and she slipped but managed not to fall. Half suspended and very scared, she heard his worried voice:

'What are you doing there, young lady? Have you decided to pay me a visit? Can't you see it is dangerous? Luckily the distance is not so big… otherwise…'

He started laughing.

She was very embarrassed and she could hardly climb back.

'Please, excuse me, I did not mean to spy on you if that is what you think… I was just walking and I slipped.'

'No, I did not think that but it is dangerous enough and this place seems to not be the most perfect place for a walk. And you scared me to death. But I think we should talk in a low voice, somebody could be sleeping.'

'I have always enjoyed sitting on roofs or on treetops and to be honest, I was curious to look on the terrace.'

'What did you expect to see, a beast or a prince? Everything is exactly the way you left, except my presence.'

'I should not have done it and I am sorry for disturbing you.'

'You did not disturb me at all. In fact, I wanted to find a moment to be alone with you but I do not know how to start telling you some things. They are not the most pleasant, on the contrary, they are very serious.'

'If you refer to your asking me to cook, I do not mind it because I suspect something and referring to the secret, I promise to keep it.'

'And what exactly is Miss Magi suspecting?'

'I suspect you are helping someone who has no food, somebody who is very hungry and Lucy might be angry if she found out.'

'You are close to the truth. Somebody is so hungry that she is almost dying and Lucy would not be angry, she could kill us all. That is all you need to know for the moment, that somebody's life depends on your food, as well as the keeping of the secret.'

'You must be joking. Why would Lucy want to kill us only because we want to prevent somebody to die from starvation? It is your way to make me keep the secret? If I promise to keep it, you must be sure I will.'

'Unfortunately, this is the truth and only a part of it. I would like to tell you all of it but you are not ready yet and I do not even know how to start. It is a long, incredible and frightening story. Maybe it is good we met now and here because I hope I put you on alert and soon I will be needing your help when you are ready.'

'God, you succeeded to frighten me! What can be so bad that you need me? And why do you all want me to be ready as if I have to fight death?'

'You get so close to the truth. But tell me, who else wants you to be ready? It is the first time I am telling you this and there is nobody else in this isolation that could do the same.'

'You told me your story was long and incredible. My story is also long and incredible and for the time being, I can not tell it to you.'

'We reached a compromise, each one has a story that we will be listening to at the right time, let's hope, and the two of us have a secret to keep. If everything goes well, please do not forget about the food tomorrow. I think it is time for you to go to bed now and do not have walks on the roof in the middle of the night. I need you, do not forget it… Good night.'

'Yes, you are right, it is late and I must leave but I will not forget what you have just told me. Good night.'

Had she had wings, she would have flown, that's how happy she was. But a moment later, she remembered Fer was a married man. How could she forget it? In fact, what did she want? A fling? Oh, no, no way. She did not feel guilty because of her desire, she did not even think of a relationship with a married man. But there was something so unnatural about the two of them! Maybe he married an older woman for her fortune, maybe he had loved her once but something came in between them and he remained a prisoner of his consciousness. She could not understand what it was but there was something abnormal between them. She wished she had found out the truth but it seemed the time had not come yet. She went to sleep and kept replaying the words "I need you, don't you forget that…"

The Dream

She felt she was ready, strong, right, that nothing could change her desire to learn the magic charm. The lane was empty but full of life. She no longer felt that horror like before. On the contrary, it was a part of her, she had merged with the Creator and a new world was taking shape, pure, clean, and perfect. She was ready to pass suffering and disease through her body, the hope without which life gets lost. Magi was ready to confront death.

First, she heard some whispers she could not understand coming from all directions, blending like babblings, then the evening fell and a stinging coldness pinched her body to keep her awake. An evening like a quiet sea was setting, then the earth started to rumble slowly, farther away, then closer, so close that if she was thrown upwards like a ball, then a hand caught her and put her in place. A new and fresh force was flowing through her body, growing up like a giant who was getting possession of the planet. She knew that everything was happening in her mind and body, she became the Sorcerer, the Healer, the powerful holder of the secret of the magic cure.

She passed in a trance over the water, over the stream at the gate, and at that moment, the Sorcerer arrived, her grandfather. He looked so tired as if he was a shadow, a spectrum, only his eyes were burning with satisfaction and full of kindness.

He had one last effort to make before the ground received him, to hand over the magic charm. She saw her grandfather's look for the last time and the next moment she felt it deep in her mind, murmuring. The countdown started, she had to learn everything by heart on the spot.

They (the name of the person you get the cure for) set off.

From home, from dinner,

Fine and beautiful

Fat and healthy,

Went till noon

And met nine witches

It struck to death

Do not sing (the name of the person)

Do not wail

That I will put a spell on you

With a copper knife

The sickness I will cure

And take it to the sea,

I will leave it there

To die forever

Like the dew

Of the Holy Sun,
Like whisper on the lane,
Ptuu!!! Ptuu!!! Ptuu!!!

Then sprinkle the person and give them a drink of water. Here
the voice in her mind faced away, feeling it again like a jerk and

with a last effort, she heard: "To make the cure stronger it must necessarily be gathered by a man, but not any man, he must be chosen and guided by the Sorcerer who will be able to send him the magic charm over a river and only once." Then a deep silence fell and on the place where the Sorcerer was. She saw an aura glittering in rainbow colors and she knew that her grandfather had finally found his eternal peace. She fell into a deep sleep and in the morning, she woke up like a new human being, a traveler between two worlds, a messenger bringing health. What message did her grandfather want to send her about that man, to trust that man, who could he be? There was no man in this isolation except for Fer. To trust him, being a stranger of her native places, and him not knowing the power and wisdom of the magic charms and the faith in the magic of nature, of the universe, of the Creator... How could she make him believe in such things? However, her grandfather had come back to tell her that it was only she who could choose and guide, it was the ultimate effort before death and at the right moment, she would be able to choose. Him.

Today was the day when she had to cook too and she was hopeful that Lucy would not be around, so she would not have to lie. However, she wouldn't give herself away, especially after what Fer had told her but she felt much better if she didn't have to give any explanations.

Lucy seemed like a ghost, keeping everybody at distance, she barely ate, she was restless, tensed as if she could not find her place. Magi did not know her whereabouts, the property was big enough, that was what she had told her, surrounded by a fence like the horses' pen and there was a notice at the entrance warning you not to trespass and that it was private property. It must be wonderful to be the owner of such a huge piece of land but it seemed they did not care. Today she had to work a lot so she banished Lucy from her mind. She made some soup from a big piece of veal with lots of vegetables and a fruit pudding and took them to Fer's kitchen. She was happy that she was alone all day long, doing everything she had planned and so she retired to her room.

Lucy felt a little better after increasing her drug dose but she knew it was only an illusion and the effects were devastating. She wandered through the forest and up the hills trying to compose herself and concentrate on what she had to do. Lately, her mind was playing tricks on her, her father appearing and reproaching her for not being as strong as before, letting herself get subjugated and touched by beautiful memories that were weakening her desire to go up to the end. Why should he scold her? He, the woeful, the traitor, the coward, coming to teach her what revenge meant. A fire was burning inside her like her stepmother. After taking her out of the grave, half-rotten but still alive, she raised the pile so beautifully that she wanted to burn down together with her. God, how beautiful the flames were, playing on the witch's body and how nicely she was whining with her last powers! It was a pity she died so soon but as long she was lying in the grave, she had time enough to relive her life, especially because she used to remind her every day. "Don't you ever forget, not even in hell, the life you lived on earth, and especially do not forget me…" And now Lucy's father was coming to remind her of what she had done! He who had done nothing while he was alive! Oh yes, he did something, he wove a spider web where Lucy and Fer were caught up and when he realised there was no escape, he disappeared. And now he was coming to ask back his love, not one but all, to get enough of it. "When do you think you will be satisfied? I can not give you all of them, you must stop!!! Or, maybe only I can stop you, you are too greedy, I am fed up with seeing you begging and running after it! Ok, I will give it to you but please do not cry, I want you to disappear forever, do you understand? I want you to get it and leave so I can leave, too, I want to find my peace." She said to herself. Then the image of her stepmother and the bald man appeared to play tricks on her and her father. She heard the voice of her stepmother. "Come and join the game, what a pity your father can not see the treasure he has and how close we are, what a united and happy family we are. If I drugged him a little, maybe he would join the game, what do you say, shall we try?" Her stepmother and the bald man were so sick they needed medicine to cure them. She had to take it out of them because they were possessed so she had no choice. The bald man was sick because of his penis so she had to extirpate it, her stepmother was possessed by the devil and only the purifying fire could save her, but not before confessing her sins. Lucy and her father watched her burn and scream with pain but she could not stop him. He wanted her back, what a sinful man but he was her father and she could not let him suffer so she would give her to him for the last time.

Lately, as usual, Fer appeared late at night waiting for Lucy to fall asleep. He prepared everything, took the keys, and hurried to the mine. He approached the girl in the cell and started to talk to her. When she looked up, he saw her timid and hopeful smile. He showed her the food but this time she did not need encouragement and started to eat by herself. She seemed to be on death row and whose last wish was fulfilled. He checked and treated the wounds, encouraged her, caressed her, and finally, he heard her voice. A thank you so faint as if it was her last breath. He asked her not to make any effort, he had to thank her for being alive and ask for her forgiveness but for the time being there were other more important things to be done. He took the ladder and went down the shaft with the rest of the food. He touched the pile of skin and bones, terrified at the thought of her being dead. He knew she found it hard to move, that this was the only position she could feel the fresh air and he was afraid she would not make it. He looked towards the niche and he noticed the food had disappeared so he felt relieved. He caressed her back, she tried to sit straight but she needed help. She was so weak and helpless but willing to live that he started to cry. Looking at him, her eyes were encouraging him, helping him to get strength because he was their only hope. He took care of her wounds, placed the food in the niche, left the water and promised to come back. He left everything as he had found it, he put the keys in their place and went to his room. He could not sleep because he was thinking of a rescue mission. He remembered Magi and the fact that they had to meet so that he could explain everything to her, especially because she was close to following the other two girls. What kind of torture did Lucy have prepared for her and how could he find out? He repaired torture devices but she had never asked for one. He had never used one as it was just a hobby, a way to pass the time. He was very sad about what he had found, he had to fight the evil but when the evil was your sister, the only one who was next to you your whole life, who helped and protected you, you do not know what to do or how to start. The thought of hurting her terrified him. Of course, he loved her, she was his sister, his only relative, and their love should have been a normal and healthy love, the one that must exist between the members of a family. Sometimes he hated her authority, the fact that she had him tied to her, being her universe. Some other times he tried to understand her, hating himself for not responding with the same love.

When Lucy woke up, she knew the time had come. She was worried a little by the resistance of the two girls. Then she thought it would be the moment of supreme triumph to sacrifice the three of them at the same time. The story had to end that way, all for one, it would be her last gift to her father. In the mine, she found a place with soft ground and she was sure she would be able to dig the grave without any help, even if it would take longer. She would have to prepare Fer not to be surprised at Magi's disappearance. She would tell him she went away because she did not feel well and could not bear solitude. So the next days would be divided between the mine and Magi and at night, she would have to sleep to regain her forces. Content with these thoughts she went down to the kitchen.

'Good morning, as busy as a bee, this means to be a compliment. I can see you know everything, I do not have to teach you and I am glad.'

'Thanks for the compliment but it is normal to know how to do the housekeeping. Will you have a cup of coffee?'

'Of course, I will and if you do not mind, I will have it right here with you. We have not spoken for a while and I need a little company.'

'That is good, it means you have recovered from the nervous breakdown.'

'A little nervous. Who told you I had a nervous breakdown?'

Then realizing her voice tone she added.

'There was not a nervous breakdown. I had some problems to manage and I had to be alone.'

Realizing she had almost given herself away, Magi said.

'Nobody told me, but I saw you sad, avoiding everybody and I thought... anyway, I am glad you have solved your problems.'

'If there is a will there is a way but let's forget it. Tell me about yourself, the way you adapted, how you spend your free time and if you like this place.'

'The place is rather isolated but its beauty makes you forget it and most of the time, usually in the evening, I walk in the forest. I would like to go shopping with you from time to time for a change.'

'I will think about your suggestion, especially since you are the only person I can take with me.'

They both laughed as if it was a good joke and continued to talk in the same tone. Lucy was around Magi all morning but tried not to pay her attention. As long as she was there, Fer would not appear and she was anxious to ask him about those miserable people. Lucy might find out at last about the diminishing supplies as she cooked so much. But she could not leave anybody to starve, they should find a solution. Finally, Lucy thought it was time for her to go to the mine to start digging, to check on her victims and take them the survival food. From the terrace, Fer watched Lucy heading towards the forest, carrying some tools that worried him but till late at night, he could do nothing. He went down to the kitchen hoping to find Magi.

'Hello, I did not mean to startle you but I am so glad I can talk to you.'

'Good to see you too, I wanted to ask you about those hungry people. I am glad I can cook for them but I am afraid your wife would ask about the missing supplies.'

'Not the best medicine can cure her. But I want to ask you something very important.'

Magi turned in amazement. She felt a kind of strain in his voice, preceding something severe, a worry, a threat hovering in the air. Seeing her so tensed made him come closer to her to calm her down but at that moment a force pushed them into one another's arms. They found themselves chained, electrified, burned by a passion that left them breathless and worried them.

It was as if they no longer existed, only the vibration of love was heard. Cut off from reality, they were looking into each other's eyes, and could see nobody but themselves. Magi made the first sign of recovery and slightly moved away from his arms.

'It seemed you wanted to ask me something.'

Fer was watching her so passionately, penetrating her entire body.

'It seems to me...'

Then as if waking from a dream he gathered all his strength and asked:

'Magi, do you trust me? I must know a lot of things might depend on it.'

'At this moment, I feel I can trust you totally but there are moments when I doubt it. You have to remember you are a married man and I can never accept a fling. There are many things I doubt, the strange relationship between you, the children you claim to have but I have not seen, the way you behave, your sickness, all these things should make me not trust any of you. How should I trust only you, then?'

'Because the time will come when you have to choose, a lot depends on it, the lives of some persons and our lives too. There are some things I cannot tell you unless you trust me. I wish I told you so many things but I prefer not to tell you for fear you would not believe me. I could start by showing you but you must be ready to face reality.'

'Lately, whenever you talk to me you frighten me, you get me ready for something but you cannot tell me what. I am a tough person, I do not lose my mind so easily so if you want to tell me or show me something dreadful, I promise to control myself.'

'Look, this is how we shall do it. Tonight, after Lucy had fallen asleep, I want you to meet me at the oak at the edge of the forest and I shall show you something to test your resistance. Maybe this has to be the beginning of the story. I want it to be the end but I have to start with it so I can tell you the beginning.'

'I will be there after 12 o'clock because I want to understand this place, this family, what can be so frightening. By the way, do I have to cook?'

'I wish but we must not catch anybody's attention so I will take whatever I find in the fridge. Taking her hands into his, he looked her deep in her eyes but he was afraid to get closer because he knew he would not let her go.'

Once she had arrived at the mine, Lucy checked on the witches, threw them the bread and water but she noticed they did not rush on it like starving wolves. They looked better than before! She thought it was the courage before death. It did not matter anyway because the time was running out and except for her, nobody knew this secret. She went to the chosen place and started digging. If everything went well, she would be ready in a few days. It was evening when she stopped. She put everything away and rushed home. She had to have a shower and find Fer to complain about Magi as if she wanted to leave them as the others did.

Fer was feeling the same, that he needed to meet his sister so when she knocked on the door, he had the feeling that she had read his mind and caught him off guard and that intimidated him.

'You did not expect me to pay you a visit at this time of the day, did you?'

'You are so surprised that you make me think it was someone else you were waiting for…'

She laughed and hugged her brother in a different way, like after a long breakup.

'Let me look at you because I have neglected you lately, I was caught up by my problems. I was selfish but there are bad times, too.'

'Indeed you avoided me but I am used to your whims and you know very well that I like loneliness.'

'It is about the loneliness here that I want to talk about. Have you seen Magi lately? I asked her if she liked the place here, how she got used to living here and if she had any problems. She said everything was ok but she feels too isolated, loneliness is depressing her and she would like to be in a place ... let's say full of life.'

'She did not seem to have such kind of problems but I did not talk to her and I cannot tell my opinion. If you say so, it must be that way.'

'My dear, it is not I who says so. She would prefer to be in a more normal place – as she said – with more people around. She even asked me to take her shopping again when I go because she had such a good time. I told her if she can not adjust she is free to leave anytime. We cannot oblige her to stay.'

'I have the feeling that none of the girls could get used to this place, that is why I asked you not to bring others because we can manage.'

'You know I like everything to be clean and I do not like to do the housework. I hoped that finally, I could find one girl to stay. You are right, if Magi leaves I shall never bring another one. It is late, I will go to bed because I have a busy day tomorrow.'

Fer's heart was pounding so hard that he was afraid he might give himself away. That is why she came, to prepare Magi's disappearance. It meant she felt something because with the other one she simply said she had left, without any other explanations.

'You know I do not care if they stay or leave, I leave these little inconveniences to you. Good night.'

He said in such a self-assured manner that he was amazed. When she closed the door behind her, he jumped so high from his chair that he almost touched the wall with his head. "God, I must hurry up and I do not know where to start. Give me the power to do everything right and stop this insanity, show me the way I must follow, I need a sign from you." He said and went out on the terrace to smoke and calm down and let the time pass until his meeting with Magi. Lucy was always sleeping with the lights on, so he was lucky not to grope in the dark and find the keys. He still heard noises in her room so he pricked his ears harder.

After having a shower, Magi was in her room, thinking about her grandfather, about what he had said about a man she would have to choose and trust in order to initiate him in the secrets of magic charm. Today Fer asked her to trust him because he was going to show her something, something that would change her destiny or the destinies of other beings. As far as she understood she had to have a strong heart and soul to resist facing reality. She had created so many scenarios that she ended up changing him into a vampire and she was the beauty who was going to save him with the help of the magic charm, the magic cure. She burst into laughter when she realised how far her imagination had gone. She started to translate the magic charm because if a man was needed, Fer was the only one here. She was trying to find the most suitable words to stick to the original form when she realised how late it was and that she had to go to meet him. She dressed up in dark clothes not to be spotted in the night, put on some sneakers, and snuck out through the back door till the oak at the edge of the forest. It was 12.30 and there was no trace of Fer so she started waiting.

Night had fallen a long time ago but Fer had to wait a while until the noises in Lucy's had room died down. Meanwhile, he had made some consistent sandwiches, took the water and some medicine, put them in the backpack, and slowly he entered Lucy's room. At that moment Lucy woke up and watched him lovingly.

'Daddy, daddy, have you come to say good night to me? I missed you, I love you but lately, you do not care much about me.'

She said in a little girl's voice. Fer was stunned. He was ready to justify himself but he realised she was living in the past, in another world, living the break-up with their father again. How much must she have loved him that she could not part with him, not after such a long time? He was so shocked that he had no reaction in the first seconds, but coming to himself he regained his role.

'Why don't you say anything? I did not want you to get angry with me when I told you about stepmother, I will never do it again because I don't want you to be unhappy. All I want is you to love me as much.'

'Daddy is not angry with you, you are my little precious girl.'

Fer tried to remember the words their father used to pamper her, to concentrate, and make no mistake.

'My princess, I have come to kiss you and say good night.'

'Good night, daddy, I love you…'

Fer got closer to the bed, kissed her forehead, and whispered slowly.

'Sleep, my little angel, daddy is with you.'

He saw her happily shutting her eyes and falling asleep. He was so touched by what had happened that he remained on the bed side, watching his sister. Discouraged, pitiful, he felt so helpless in front of this grief, this trauma that he wanted to give everything up and hide in his cave forever. He caressed her hair. Her facial features were so relaxed that he was sure she was with their father. He wondered if he should go on with what he had started or abandon everything and indulge in the present life. He was caught in the middle, balancing between two worlds, the past on one hand and the present with his sister who was sick with grief and the girls in the mine. Then it was Magi whom he started to love, he was sure of it, and another life he would have liked to live. But wasn't it selfishness to fight against Lucy and sacrifice her, wasn't he saving himself, his consciousness, his life? His mind and body remained untouched by any vice because of her, she was the front line soldier who got all the beatings. His sister was sick, she could be mad, she needed help, hospital, doctors, he had to help her... Maybe it was better to meet Magi, to tell her the truth, to find a solution, he could not abandon anybody, they all needed help. He closed the door, took the backpack and headed towards the meeting place.

Magi was ready to leave when she heard a noise in the grass. She stood there waiting, but she hid behind a bush not to be seen in case it was not Fer. When she saw Fer, she came out angry for making her wait.

'Finally, you decided to show up! I thought it was a joke or you had forgotten.'

'I was ready to abandon everything, I am caught in the middle but too many lives depend on me, on my decision, so here I am. Follow me because we are short of time and I will tell you some things on the way.'

'Where do you want to take me in the middle of the night? Do you think I am so naïve to go with you?'

'If I had wanted to hurt you I would have had 100 opportunities because you go walking in the forest every night. I do not need a date, did you not think of it? I want you to come with me to the mine, to prove to you I am right.'

'You may be right but I am not completely reassured...'

'Please Magi, we don't have mch time, make up your mind, will you come or not? I do not want to pressure you or oblige you but you must decide now.'

'Ok, let's go and I want to listen to what you want to tell me.'

He took her by the hand and pulled her towards the mine.

'The first thing you must know is that Lucy and I are not husband and wife but sister and brother. No, do not stop because it is already too late. I am sorry I was so blunt but there was no other way to tell you. The idea belongs to my sister, of course. After some happenings in our life or better said, her life. You must know that my sister is very sick, she was in the past too, when she found out that our father, whom she loved so much, was found hanged. She spent one year in hospital and when she came back she was a different person. Here we are. I will continue my story some other time because now comes the real challenge for you. I want you to know that it knocked me down when I saw what I shall show to you so it does not matter what your reaction is because I will understand.'

He was squeezing her hand so hard while pulling her that the moment they arrived she was not able to say a word.

'There is no other way to make you understand, except starting from here. No matter how hurt you will be hurt by watching this, please, stay calm, do not run because that was what I wanted to do in the first moment. You may manifest yourself in any way but try to pull yourself together because somebody needs us desperately and someone dear to me needs help more desperately.'

Magi nodded her head, implying she was ready to enter that place. In the light of the torch she saw some old galleries and a smell of closed space and mould struck her. Opening a second door, Fer stopped, put down his backpack, and came to her. He embraced her so that she felt his emotion. He wanted to encourage her, to strengthen her for what was coming. He lit a bigger torch light which spread light all over the place and told Magi to get closer to the jail. Dumbfounded, she watched a chained creature who was almost naked, with her body full of wounds and what was left of her being her bones and eyes. Her hair was very dirty, she stank so horribly as if one open mouth of hell was throwing out the most disgusting things. Magi felt a claw stinging her stomach and heart. Her mouth contracted spasmodically, wanting to cry for fear but no sound came out and the next moment she fainted. Fer, who was next to her and was watching her reactions, grabbed her before she touched the ground. He sprinkled her with water and massaged her temples. When she opened her eyes she threw herself to his chest, screaming.

'I know what you are going through, crying gets the pressure out.'

He caressed her. She was afraid to get away from his arms and to watch again, to believe that everything was real. She did not know how to face the moment when she was no longer at his chest. He took her arms that were squeezing him like a screw vice and made her understand this was not all, there was another creature in a worse condition and without their help, she might not survive. Magi hardly managed to compose herself but she could not move. She saw Fer approach the girl, feed her and then treat her wounds. Her mind started to think, she stood up and came to Fer.

'I am better now and I would like to help you.'

He turned to her said.

'Try and talk to the girl until I finish with her wounds. If she sees a new face she will be convinced that we want to help her and she will hang on longer.'

Magi stood in front of the girl and watched her eating as if not chewing, then she drank a bit to help her swallow. Magi waited until the girl had finished the first sandwich, then she tried to remove the hair from her eyes and communicate with her. Magi felt her hand on her arm as if to stop her but it was just a way of speaking. I could find no word of encouragement but she looked in my eyes and a connection of trust was established between us.

'I am sorry but we have to go to the other girl.'

Feeling awful, she left her hands and followed Fer.

Fer opened a lid, put a ladder in, and made a sign to follow him. Watching the shaft lit by the torchlight, she realised she had reached the realm of shadows and death. The smell made her stomach turn, she started to vomit, her eyes were in tears and she started to suffocate. Fer gave her a mask for her nose and mouth and told her to help him. There was a skeleton covering some plastic bottles, half sunken in a gutter full of creatures. He showed Magi the wall opening where some fresh air was coming in and the niche next to it. They lowered to help her and Magi felt her participation in their effort. Fer was ecstatic. The girl's face was a skeleton used in the anatomy classes with a strength that was shook you. She reached for food and Fer gave her some soup too, knowing she lost all her teeth. While eating she watched them in turns for fear that they could vanish. Magi witnessed the scene helplessly, discovering a new Fer, full of compassion, giving them hope and she knew he was the chosen one who would have to accomplish the real cure. She was so moved by his delicacy as if he was handling expensive china that could break any time. After he had left her some food and assured her that everything was going to end, they climbed up, shut everything, and left.

'We have no time for discussions now, we must go home and put the keys in their place. Imagine what could happen if she did not find them.'

The discovery marked Magi profoundly and she followed him quietly, realising the danger he was exposed to. She started to understand a little but most of the story was unknown to her and she was anxious to find out everything. How could things go so far? What pushed Lucy to such macabre things? Magi knew that Fer would tell her all now that Pandora's box was opened. In front of the house, he told her to wait for him until he had placed the keys back. It was 4 a.m. but none of them felt the time fleeting. When Fer came back, he told Magi that his sister was sleeping and for the rest of the time he was going to tell her what he thought was more important. It was such an unbelievable story and she had heard only a part of it but she believed each word that he uttered.

'I am sorry you have to go through all this but it is the only way to save us all, including her. Tonight we shall meet again and I will try to find out what she has planned for you. She warned me that you want to leave us and this made me understand you are going to be the next victim and the only way to make you trust me was a brutal one, to make you face reality. You must make the effort and be self-controlled when facing her because she senses the smallest change. If not, all that I succeeded to accomplish will fall apart. If you feel you are not capable to face her, tell her you are sick, only do not give us away. There was no time for other words so we hurried to our rooms.'

Magi sat on the bed with her clothes on. She was numb, her ears were buzzing and her whole body was shaking. She felt as if she had woken in the middle of a horror movie. The images in the mine mixed with Fer's story panicked her and clouded her judgement. She wanted to change her clothes and get some hours of sleep but she was so exhausted that she could not move. Why her? To be caught in this game of revenge? She could not believe it was happening to her. Finally, exhausted, she fell asleep. She woke up terrified by her own cry. She was wet with perspiration, her clothes stuck to her body and sweat drops were covering her forehead.

She looked around with horrified eyes, then lay down on the pillow to recover. Was it a dream or reality? She could see an inert body, tied up, that Lucy was carrying. She saw the grave and realised that the body was hers. When Lucy dumped her in the grave, she screamed so hard that she woke up. Her breath was irregular as if breathing for the last time. She calmed down but remained in bed, being too disturbed by her dream. She took off her wet clothes, took her dressing gown, and went to have a shower. She looked tired, her face was pale and her body was weak.

Lucy had been awake for a long time and was wondering why Magi did not show up. She drank her coffee and was waiting for her not for the pleasure of being with her but to enjoy her victim. Lately, her father was visiting her more often, he was probably missing her. She even saw him coming to her room to say good night. That night she was ecstatic. He told her he was not angry with her, that he loved her so much annd said "My princess, daddy is with you."

How long was it since she had heard those words? Before she came, the nanny, the witch, the demon sent to destroy their love, the dragon who lured him with her lascivious body and hypnotic calls... "Forgive me Father, for not being with you up to the end but I did not know how to protect you. I thought it was good entering her game but I let myself be corrupted and I disappointed you. I tried to fight but you were so upset with me, you would no longer come and caress my hair and kiss me good night and maybe it was the revenge of a little girl tired of waiting for you. But I was only a child who was longing for you... Soon we will be together again, this time I will come to you and say goodbye." She said. Suddenly she stood up and went to her room. Since Magi covered the mirrors in her room, she had to wait for the moment she was in the shower. She opened the mirror when Magi entered. What was happening to her, why was she looking so tired and pale? She hoped Magi was not coming down with something right now, she would not change her plans but she wanted her to be powerful. Lucy would wait for her in the kitchen and find out what was going on, after that, she would go to the mine. She could not postpone any longer, she wanted so much to be with her father, to be in his protective arms once again.

Magi did not know how to cope with the day. She wanted to tell Lucy she was sick. The best way was to pretend to be just before her menstruation and changing the climate may influence the organism. She really felt sick so she wouldn't have to pretend so she would be able to retire to her room sooner. Why did Fer warn her about the mirrors? 'No matter what happens, keep the mirrors covered, make sure every time that they are perfectly covered', he had said. She would have to go upstairs, no matter what, she thought encouragingly. However, seeing Lucy in the kitchen, she had a moment of hesitation, she was ready to turn back and run but Fer's words were in her ears: 'All I have succeeded to accomplish will collapse.' Lucy's eyes were searching her but in the last moment, she directed to her with a tired smile.

'I must apologise for being late but you know what it means to be a woman. I think the change affected my period, I have a headache and back pains that I could hardly get up. Maybe you have some medicine for this?'

'Do not worry. It happens to me too when I travel. Here is the medicine cabinet and this is exactly what you need.'

Magi took the pills with water.

'You saved me, I feel shivery because of pains. I will do my duty, of course, and I will go to my room earlier.'

'I know you will catch up with things even if you do not do the housework today. You may go now if you are not feeling well. I will be missing all day long because I have some business to take care of.'

She left the kitchen completely calm.

Feeling weak, Magi sat down on a chair and felt her body shivering. All the power gathered to face this meeting was leaving her, she was holding on to the chair not to fall and her eyes were full of tears. She could see the mine, the two girls, she could see her body dumped in the grave... She squeezed the chair harder not to break into a fit of hysteria. She remained like that with tears rolling down her cheeks, waiting for this moment to pass because she was feeling so weak and vulnerable.

In the mine, Lucy did not pay attention to the girls but she started digging immediately. It is not easy for a woman to dig a hole but she was happy thinking that soon everything would be over. At the end of one gallery, she discovered a cave that was perfect for the last stage. It was spacious, high and there was a small island in the middle. It was surrounded by a thin stream of water, clean as a mirror. After measuring it, she marked 3 places where she would place the 3 funeral piles for the 3 witches. The middle one was destined for Magi, the last would be the first, accompanied by the other two who were dying anyway and would not need so much fire. This was the sign, the sign sent by her God, everything was at hand. "Search and you will find," It was so simple, she knew she was directed here to accomplish his work.

'To the fire with the witches!!!'

She was turning round and round bursting into screams that invaded the mine.

Fer woke up after he had slept like a log. He had a shower and did not hear the slightest noise when he went downstairs. The first moment he saw Magi, he felt that everything was lost, that she could not cope with his sister and the plan failed. He approached her, took her from the chair, and squeezed her to his chest. He cared no longer for anything, for life, girls, his sister, he only wanted her he get stuck on him.

'It's ok, it's ok.'

He gently encouraged her.

'I will find a solution for all this. Please come to your senses because I do not want to go further without you.'

Feeling her trembling from being cold, he took her to his room in his arms. He put her on the bed and covered her but she seemed to be far away. He lay down next to her and started rubbing her cold hands until he felt her hot lips on his neck. They were so soft and hot that he lost his self-control. Her hands were in his hair trying to pull him towards her, desperately looking for his lips and her feet crossing his feet. He was pulsating from head to toe, he was burnt up by the passion of touching her, finding out her mystery, there was so much pain in their love, a cast that could no be broken not even by death. In the moment of supreme connection, the sky and the earth disappeared and a new being was born, a new beginning, and love and hope was born out of desperation and hatred.

For hours on end, they could not get loose, they were afraid the time would be too short, they could not stop the explosion in their bodies. The euphoric charge they shared was so intense that they managed to stop only towards the evening. Scared by this devouring desire, conscious that Lucy might catch them at any moment, they parted knowing they would meet again at night. They were no longer afraid of anything and anybody, they were endowed with something new, something that was worth fighting for, something called love.

Fer finally understood the meaning of the word love. If you would have to die for it, he was ready. She was the beginning and the end, the eyes, the soul, and his desire to live. Lying on the bed, he savored the smell and he got lost in her again and again. But the end had just started and he barely got up, opened the window to let the fresh air enter in case his sister paid him a visit. He arranged the bed and lit a cigarette that he smoked on the spot where Magi had lain and fallen asleep.

Lucy was admiring the grave. It was deep enough for the body, only the head could remain outside. She would keep her a few days without food and water to weaken her and then she would drag her to the funeral pile, place her next to the others, light a small spark and everything would disappear. Tomorrow she would start making the 3 funeral piles. She had everything she needed to be ready in a few days. She no longer felt tired, that's how satisfied she was with her work. It was late, she needed food, a shower, and a good night's sleep. Lately, she had not kept her diary updated and that was not good. When she would be next to her father, she wanted the diary to be left to Fer so he would know everything that had happened and understand that all she did was only for love, the love that should connect a real family and no obstacle should exist. She would not justify her deeds, they are not the side effects of her illness but of a malady existing in life, of debauchery that got out of control, of people's hypocrisy and infamy. She was not sorry for what she had done but she was sorry for what she had not done. She succeeded to exterminate a small part and the rest would be hanging on humanity until someone else would continue her work. She no longer wanted to wait, she missed her father and she knew he loved her.

Fer woke up when he heard noises in Lucy's room. It was the moment to wake up and wait. He thought about Magi and what had happened between them. He could no longer harness his desires, they grew bigger and bigger, invading his body, soul, and mind. He longed to keep her stuck on him, to feel that explosion that made them both disappear in one another, in a world full of ecstasy and fulfillment. If this was what his father had felt while being with his stepmother, then it was no wonder he committed suicide. Fer could not be with her or without her. He remembered the saying "oh, love, you can make a man out of a beast and sometimes a beast out of a man." He felt it at this moment, that he could become a beast if somebody touched his love. It was late already but Lucy did not go to bed, nor did she come for a visit. He was worried because of it but he could not go to her, he would have aroused suspicions so all he could do was be on the watch. He could not even cook because he never knew what to expect from her. What if she decided to come and see him before going to bed?

He made some coffee and went out on the terrace to wait.

After having a shower and something to eat, Lucy started to fill in her diary. The more she described the suffering her victims were enduring, the bigger her madness became. She wanted to get all these witches, family destroyers, malefic beings together and set them on fire. Maybe she could attract the attention of the world of the danger they represent. However, she was satisfied enough by punishing a few, at least. She was not thinking of Fer lately, maybe because she felt the presence of her father more intensely than ever before. He followed her all over the place, guided her, watched over her sleep, so she took the drug to be with him again.

Fer entered Lucy's room, approached her bed, and caressed her. His heart sank at the sight of the smile that lit her face and heard her talking to her father. He took the keys and rushed to the meeting point. They jumped into one another's arms and got lost in endless kisses.

'We have no time for us now but later may be better, I cannot promise anything.'

'I know, my dear, I want nothing except to be with you and help you. I must tell you a story as incredible as yours. Your sister is sick and maybe we can help her. I hope with all my heart we can.'

The first thing he did in the mine was take care of the girls. Both were in better condition and they understood that they would save them soon.

'We must look around, maybe we shall find a clue connected to you and her plans.'

'I want to tell you something. I dreamed about Lucy dragging me and throwing me in a hole. I woke up screaming.'

'Do not think about it now. It is natural to dream like that after everything you have seen. Let's not waste our time and look around.' More galleries led from that point so Fer had to decide which one to follow.

'We should find some traces left by Lucy. That is what we shall be looking for.'

They followed the footprints left by Lucy on the ground and stopped horrified on the edge of a hole. Magi saw herself dragged and dumped into that hole. So her dream was a warning for what was going to happen.

'Magi, I think you were right. Somebody beyond death and who loves you and watches over you sent you that dream so you can defend yourself. It is good to know that somebody is up there… For the time being, we cannot do much but at least we know and we will try to prevent it. Remember that I am with you. I have never known what love meant, what it means to be really happy and now I must tell you. You must know in case something happens or goes wrong and I or we do not survive.'

'Magi, I, Richard, love you with all my heart! No matter what happens, I want to live with you, I cannot live without you. As long I am here next to you, do not be afraid of anything or anybody. There is nothing except death that could set us apart. I will not give you up, I will fight for you.'

So Fer's real name was Richard. He seemed like a knight from a fairy tale, he was giving off power, courage, self-control. Fer the shy, the timid, the weak had disappeared, he was the real master of her life.

'Richard, I love you, I could not conceive life without you, no matter what our fate is. I will be where you are and as long as you are next to me and alive, I will be next to you and alive. If you pass into the world of shadows my shadow will follow you to be together for eternity.'

The vows they exchanged at that moment and place united them forever and strengthened their desire for what was coming. It was fate that wanted them to be together on a dangerous road where love would be tested.

'I will go on calling you Fer to not give us away. You said before that somebody from beyond this world loves me and you are right. Here is the story I must tell you connected to my grandfather, a magic charm, a medicine that can cure any disease.'

'It is late, I think we should postpone everything for tomorrow. I promise I will listen to you tomorrow night, now it is better to hurry up.'

'Magi! Did you leave the light on in the kitchen? I think we have a problem.'

'No, I did not, it means only one thing, Lucy is awake. You said she had taken the drug.'

'She probably took a smaller dose or her body does not react as well as before. No matter what it is, the most important thing is that she must not know we were gone together. She is used to me walking at night so I will enter the kitchen to see if she is there. I will make some noise, talk a little to her so you can sneak to your room through the back door.'

'What about the keys? What if she had discovered them missing?'

'I hope she did not so I can put them back in their place. Let us not waste time. You go round the house to get in through the back door and I will go through the front.'

Fer entered the house like a man having nothing to hide and went directly to the kitchen. Lucy sat with a cup of tea and stared at him suspiciously.

'How come you woke up so early?'

'Why wouldn't I, do you mind? Did you resume your walkings or did you find company?'

'Honestly, many times I wished I had company but I did not know where to find it. You took care of that.'

'And what did you want, to leave you at the hand of a whore and be like father, to lose your mind and me being abandoned again? And now, this woman with such a strange name, Magi! If I were not attentive you would hook up with her.'

He was ready to contradict her in a tough way but at Magi's name he almost lost control. He had to find out if she had found out something, so he said calmly:

'What happened to you all of a sudden? Didn't you tell me she was ready to leave? And I do not know what you mean about hooking up with her. Have I ever done such a thing?'

'I caught you a few times watching her in a certain way, the way father looked at stepmother. Do you think I am blind? I can see and understand more than 1000 eyes, do not forget it.'

Fer turned his back on her and went upstairs. He was boiling mad, he wanted to fight back but it was not the right time. He hoped Magi had succeeded in sneaking back to her room. On the first floor he stopped, Lucy's room was ajar. He entered and put the keys in their place just in time because he heard Lucy coming upstairs.

Magi was standing at the window and she could hear their voices as if they were arguing. It was time she sneaked down to the basement. When she entered her room, she could hardly control her emotions. She changed her clothes and went to bed hoping that Fer would get over his meeting with Lucy well. Fer was not ready to confront her yet. She felt so much pain when he told her their life story, like an excuse for her deeds. However, he was ready to stop these futile cruelties and at the same time, he wanted to find a solution to help Lucy. Magi felt she was loved by this man in a different way, she found strength in him too, but he needed help as if he was made of two halves, one for his sister and the other one for her. A less painful way had to be found for him to become a single being, to merge into one single being. She knew that Lucy was very sick and she thought maybe "We the Great" could help her. For this, she had to make Fer believe in the magic charm and use it against the sickness, the evil in Lucy's soul and body.

Fer was really feeling very sick. These nights had indeed put his mind and body to the test. Finally, he found what he had always wanted, the missing part, something he had never had access to, and that was Magi.

It was early morning but Lucy had already reached the mine because she had to build the 3 funeral piles and for this, she had to dig the holes for the wooden pillars. It was nothing compared to the big hole but they had to be well pushed into the ground. Luckily, she found some wooden beams and lots of boards that could create a great fire. It would be like a carnival, like a campfire, like a holiday. She would be 33 years old but nobody was giving her gifts, flowers, champagne, etc. She made them herself. What could be more wonderful than 3 burning funeral piles, three souls purified by the living fire? She couldn't wish for more than this celebration. Not even her father had thought of such a present. She was looking forward to seeing his reaction.

After a few hours of sleep, Magi woke up pretty worried. Lately, she used to appear rather late in the kitchen and she was afraid Lucy would become suspicious. She did not know that after meeting Fer, she left for the mine again. When she went upstairs, she was happy to be alone.

Fer noticed his sister leaving for the mine and it was a bad thing. It meant she was in a hurry to apply her plan. Although he was tired, he could not sleep as he was thinking of a solution that was good for everybody. How could he make Lucy give up all this? How could he make her understand that she was sick and needed help? How could he protect Magi and help the other two girls? He would listen to Magi first, maybe that is the answer. That night they would not go to the mine, they would talk and maybe they would come up with a plan. A little calmer, he lay on the bed and fell asleep.

After working from sunrise to sunset, Lucy finished the holes and fixed the wooden beams. She stepped backward to admire her work. She was very satisfied with the way she had arranged them. They looked great as if prepared for the crucifixion. In fact, it was a kind of crucifixion but by burning. The girls did not matter anymore, they were only living corpses and she already knew how to deal with the other one.

'Everything is going according to plan so I deserve a little rest. It is good I ended it.'

After the night fell, Fer and Magi met up.

'I can hardly breathe without you, my love.'

'I go crazy thinking that we can not meet like normal people. You must listen to me because only you can make the cure. It is about Lucy and the disease that is consuming her.'

'Tonight we are not going to the mine but to my secret sanctuary to have a talk because the moment is nearer than we thought. Lucy has tried several times to discover it but she did not succeed. We are safe there.'

Reaching the secret cave, Magi was impressed by his inventiveness. Nobody could have discovered it because it was so well hidden. Inside, Fer lay down a blanket and asked Magi to tell her story.

'The first night that I arrived at your house, a sorcerer appeared in my dream to tell me that I am in a sick place, that I must defend myself but I cannot unless I make a magic potion called "We the Great" and a magic charm to accompany the potion. At first, I did not pay any attention to the dream but it came back and in time, I realized that something was happening here. The magic charm can be transmitted and learned only once and over a stream of water. The one receiving it must learn it on the spot which is the only time also. The sorcerer is non other than my grandfather, he was the last Wizard or Healer, as we call him. After he had succeeded in passing the magic charm to me, he disappeared forever. My grandfather also told me that I had to hand it over to a man who could cure and at the right time, I would know who the man is. Now I know and I am no longer afraid of anything. It is you, Fer!'

'How can you say such a thing, Magi? Look at me! I have done nothing good in my life, and I indulged in my comfort although I suspected something was happening here. I wanted to believe I was helpless because I did not want to change my lifestyle. I did not have the courage to break up with my sister, to face her and leave. I knew she was insane, I suspected her being capable of anything, even murder, but I did nothing. I am a coward and her accomplice because I did not take action and now you tell me I am the chosen one. He must be a pure soul, to be able to identify with the Creator, and suffering and sickness shall pass through his body.'

'Listen to me carefully. It does not matter what you have done in the past. I saw you kneeling in front of those girls, I could see their suffering on your face and body, how passionate you were. The way you were talking, encouraging them, you gave them back the desire to fight, resist, you gave them back their hope.'

'That is why you are the chosen one to redeem the mistakes of the past. If you are not convinced that you can do it maybe everything could be futile. I translated the magic charm but I must tell it to you over a stream of water but only when you trust yourself and you are ready. You said the time was short. Think about it and tomorrow I will wait for an answer.'

'I am not convinced I am the chosen one, I wish I could. Do not judge me, Magi, but I cannot see myself like a Sorcerer. In my opinion, he must have extraordinary powers, a native gift, a belief in the power of nature, of goodness. I have nothing of this kind, how could I be? I promise you one thing, tomorrow I will go shopping and bring you everything you need to prepare the magic cure.'

They went back home with their souls full of sadness. Magi knew he was the chosen one but he had to feel it too. She blamed herself for not telling him sooner, being afraid it could be too late. Fer felt he had failed and let her down. He felt devastated. Magi was sure he was the chosen one and the more she tried to convince him, the more he backed off. Everything seemed so fantastic, it was nothing but a dream. Maybe she had a mind full of fantasy, she dreamed about her childhood place, her grandfather, and hence the story with "We the Great." There were too many details, how the elements of nature needed to be gathered, where, by whom, how the sick person needed be treated, and that mysterious magic charm that needed be learned and said. Fer felt overwhelmed by so many mysteries but he promised Magi to think about it, maybe he would find something to catch on.

Seeing Lucy, Fer told her he wanted to go and buy some books.

'Why do you want to go today, when I am so busy?'

'I do not understand why you are so busy and why today? Today is a day like any other one. Yes, I want to go shopping today.'

'I am sorry but I cannot accompany you. You know I do not like to leave you alone but if you insist to go today, you must do it on your own.'

'I won't be too long, so I will go alone.'

Lucy had to make the last preparations. Once she reached the mine, she started to gather wood and pile it up to have everything at hand. She had enough wood, rope, scissors, a small bottle of gas not to have surprises because of the dampness. She finished the last details because the night would bring the accomplishment of her work She hurried home to change her clothes and have a little rest. She did not want to be late meeting Fer and Magi. When she entered the house, Magi was finishing her duties in the kitchen.

'I am glad to see you, but what happened to you? Your face seems as if you are under the weather. Still sick? Look, I am going to have a shower and please make me some sandwiches because I am as hungry as a wolf. Please bring them to the terrace. It is a wonderful evening and it would be a pity not to take advantage of it.'

Magi was surprised to see her in such a good mood but these were the freaks of a sick person. Sometimes she wanted to run and inform the authorities but what could she tell them? That she works illegally, that Lucy is sick, that there are two girls in the mine who are prisoners and are starving and Lucy wants to kill them... Who will believe her because nobody reported them missing and there is no suspicion. They can not trespass on a private property. She could not abandon them now, knowing the truth. Fer came back from the city but they could not meet and see if he had found everything they needed for the magic charm and now Lucy was in the mood to talk.

When Lucy came downstairs she bumped into Fer.

'What are you doing? Have you found the books you needed?'

'Yes, I found some. I wish to drink some natural orange juice.'

'Ok, come to the terrace and I will ask Magi to squeeze some oranges.'

'No thanks, I am not in the mood for company. Please bring it to me when you come upstairs.'

'Suit yourself but it is a wonderful evening and it's a pity to miss it.'

Lucy was ecstatic. Everything was going according to the plan.

'Magi, I hope you don't mind doing something more.'

'Why should I mind? That is why I am here!'

'I would like you to squeeze some oranges and make 3 glasses of juice. I met Fer before and he asked for a glass of natural orange juice. He was not in a good mood and refused to drink it with us on the terrace.'

'The juices will be ready as soon as you have finished eating. Shall I leave Fer's juice in the kitchen?'

'Yes, leave it, I shall take it up to his room.'

Magi brought the two glasses of juice and put them on the table while Lucy was finishing her last sandwich.

'Oh, my hands are dirty, I forgot the napkins!'

'I'll go to the kitchen and bring some.'

As soon as she disappeared, Lucy took a small envelope with a white powder from her pocket and poured it into Magi's juice. She put the glass back exactly when Magi came back. It was a wonderful night and Magi was anxious to meet Fer, to hear the verdict, but Lucy seemed to have been stuck on the terrace.

'When I finish my juice I will go to my room because I am very tired.'

Hearing that, Magi hurried to finish. She took everything to the kitchen and left for her room. She was feeling a kind of weakness all over her body and lay on the bed a little. She had to wait until Lucy fell asleep anyway.

After pouring the sleeping pill into Fer's juice, she went upstairs with the glass.

'Here is your long awaited glass of juice! Show me the books you have bought, what was the rush for?After checking the books on his desk, she sat down in the rocking chair to have a chat. Fer was worried about this prolonged visit but showed nothing of it.'

'How have you been feeling lately? I do not know why you avoided me.'

'Maybe yes, maybe no. Anyhow, it is not important because we both know you are not fond of my company.'

She did not want to leave until she was sure he would drink the juice. She needed him to be asleep tonight not to mess with her plans while having his night walks. When she saw the empty glass, she got up, said good night, and went to her room to wait for the sleeping pill to take effect on both of them.

Fer felt so sleepy and suddenly a thought struck him, how could he not realize? It was too late and he lay down on the bed and fell asleep.

When she heard no more noises, Lucy decided it was time for action. She pulled a little cart to the back door and went down to Magi's room. She was fast asleep. It seemed the little lady was dressed up for a walk. She tied her well, covered her with a tarpaulin, and dragged her to the cart, heading for the mine. Once in front of the hole, she dropped Magi with legs out in front. She had a little work to do because the girl had to be supported but she had thought of that too. She made a support for the armpits to keep her body up until she finished filling the hole. How nice the head was looking, supported by boards so the ground would not get into her mouth until she woke up. She wanted her alive so she was careful not to suffocate her. She did not give her a large dose of sleeping pills and soon she would wake up, her dear stepmother. A few days of slimming cure do not hurt! Everything turned out better than she expected, she said to herself while going home.

When Fer woke up, it was afternoon and he was still feeling the effect of the sleeping pills. He barely managed to drag himself to the bathroom. he filled the bathtub with cold water and waited a little to recover.

Tears were running down his cheeks but he felt nothing. It was the only place Lucy did not have the courage to enter and he needed time to gather his powers. He stayed like that until his body was frozen, then he got out and rubbed his body with a rough towel. A veil dropped off his mind and the effect of the sleeping pills disappeared completely and he knew what he had to do. He remembered their father had committed suicide when the nanny turned 33 years old. In a few days, Lucy would turn 33 so that was the clue. He had often heard his sister talking about this anniversary when she wanted to make their father a special gift. Everything was beginning to make sense so Magi might still be alive because she was the stepmother, the witch. What happens to witches? They are burned on funeral piles. "God, help me and make my reasoning be true and Magi be alive! Tonight I must enter the mine and check." He prayed to God as he had never done before to handle the situation. He drank one strong coffee and made a supernatural effort to face his sister. It was the last card he played and everything depended on how he managed to behave. Despite his repulsion, he had self – control when he faced Lucy.

'Hello Lucy, you look so fresh. In fact, I myself slept so well. I feel very energetic this morning.'

'I did not sleep very well but it is time for it too.'

'How come you are alone, do not tell me that Magi has already left, out of the blue! She did not seem ready to leave and she should have said goodbye, at least.'

'I can see you noticed her absence so soon. Do you miss her or maybe she misses you?'

'I can see the connection between us but your mind has always seen more than there is. Am I not allowed to ask?'

With a raging mind, Lucy said.

'Do not tell me what my mind can see, I see only what it is. Do you think I was blind to not see you both devouring one another with your eyes? One look was enough, although you avoided one another. Fer, you lack my experience and you cannot pretend. I am sorry for you because you must start learning from 0 at your age.'

'I am sorry for you too but I told you, you were sick and you see what it is not. You always compare me to Father or identify me with him and guard me not to fall into temptation. Do you not think I have had enough and I could burst out?'

'It is hard to believe that. I have not seen any sign of rebellion so far and trust me, I am watching you. As long as I am alive you promised not to dump me and it is obvious you still have to wait.'

'Better late than never...'

And he left because he felt like strangling her. She must have sensed something but she was not aware they knew about the mine. He could not go too far from the house and he needed to look the same. He could not go on like that, things had gone too far. And no matter how much he loved Lucy or how much he owed her, she needed to be stopped. Magi was right, only he could cure her, somebody who knew her and whom she trusts. Her death would bring no satisfaction to him but if that was the last solution, he need to accept it. He did not know if he could live after that, maybe that was the price he would pay, to give up what he had found. Yes, he was the chosen one because he knew he could give up this life and the next one.

Magi felt her body was heavy as if she was trapped in a sack and held by a burden that did not allow her arms and feet to move. She could hardly breathe. She made an effort to wake up from that horrible dream. Where was she and what was happening to her? She repeatedly thought that she was in a nightmare she could not wake up from. But her eyes were wide open. She closed her eyes and tried to remember what she had done before falling asleep. She had to meet Fer but there was some time felt so she lay down on the bed before she fell asleep. But before? It was important to remember what she had done before she reached her room. She felt a bitter taste in her mouth and saw the empty glass of juice... Yes, that was what she did, she drank orange juice which she made at Lucy's request. The taste in her mouth was like rotten eggs. Maybe she had food poisoning and that was why she was feeling so heavy and could not move. Her head was spinning and she could hardly breathe.

If she had the power to get up, drink some water, and vomit, maybe she could feel better. However it was more than that, it was as if she was buried underground... No, it was not possible and she screamed so loud that she was scared too. Such a thing could not possibly happen to her... The mine, the hole, the dream, the taste in her mouth, Lucy, Fer... All these thoughts unrolled in her mind and she started to understand. That smell of mold and of fear was everywhere and she was trapped in it, there was nothing but darkness and despair.

Lucy was on cloud nine. Finally, she had reached the end. That whore had almost hooked him again! She thought her sickness and drugs weakened her. She saw Magi watching her and trying to get into her soul. Magi pretended to be obedient, tried to satisfy all her wishes. But this time she failed because her father finally understood who she was and what she wanted and he did not stand in her way. Her whole body was vibrating with happiness, she would be her father's princess again, but this time forever.

Fer was desperate too. He spent all day long watching Lucy and walking around the mine. He hoped to find a place, a hole, an opening to squeeze in and reach Magi. Exhausted, he went back home but Lucy did not move from her room. He could hear her moving around the room, moving things, talking to herself, laughing, as if getting ready to leave. His only hope was that, once night fell, she would take the drug and he could enter the mine and save Magi and the other two girls. But all the signs showed that Lucy had not finished her work yet and if his reasoning was right, they were still alive and this was what mattered most. This thought encouraged him and made him persistent. He saw his sister only once but it seemed like she was from another world. She smiled and said: "Do not be afraid of anything, salvation is near." Then she disappeared. What he heard next was only the noises in her room. After midnight, when everything had calmed down, he entered her room but he could not find the keys in their usual place. With her hair disheveled on the pillow and with a bright face, Lucy looked like the little girl for whom every day was a celebration. But he had no time for memories, they belonged to the past. The keys were nowhere as if they had evaporated. Why would she hide them? Did she know more than she let on or did she do it as a simple precaution? Her intelligence should not be underestimated despite her sickness or maybe it was the sickness and her thirst for revenge that made her more cautious.

If this was her last moment, he could not afford any mistakes. He controlled his anxiousness and started to look for the keys methodically. He searched all the drawers, cupboards, and even the bathroom but the keys were nowhere. He could no longer concentrate, his body was shattered by sighs, he felt like he was losing his mind. He was standing in the middle of the room and he felt like rushing to Lucy, shaking her and telling her the most outrageous words, he was on the point of killing her. But he could not do that, she was his sister, blood from his blood and his duty was to help her. When their father left them in their nanny's hands, he was eternally isolated and she was the one left to face all the vices and suffering gathered in one being, so it was no wonder that she had lost her mind. As she took over all the suffering, he would have to take over all the trauma and her pain, to help her recover from her illness and beat it. It was the hardest obstacle, it was the trap set by their stepmother and their father as if determined to keep their eyes on them even after death. Maybe the magic charm that Magi brought from overseas was the miracle everybody needed. He scanned the room once more, then Lucy and hope emerged in his soul. Maybe it was not too late for any of them. Now he was sorry he had not listened to Magi and did not learn the magic charm but at that time it seemed like a fantasy as if from the legends of the world. The Sorcerer, the nature, the magic charm, the faith, he had read about them only in books. He could not believe such things could have an effect in this century but he learned one thing: if you really believe in the power of goodness, you can beat everything and now, in the 12th hour, he believed. The nature was opening its gates, all he had to do was to knock, ask for it, and believe in its powers. It was the miracle he could never have dreamed of, it was its joy to give, to heal. He would find a way to learn the magic charm because he was the real Healer. When the sun rose, he would be in the middle of nature and pick up that magic cure that would heal Lucy's body and soul and would break the charm.

When she woke up, Lucy was astonished. There was a big bunch of roses of all colors in the middle of the table and a note: Happy birthday, a little of how much I would like to give you. With Love, Fer. She started to cry happily. She sat down on the bed and laughed and cried with joy, thinking there was somebody to remember her birthday and who still loved her.

This was the real love in a family and she wanted to protect it so nobody could interfere. The bunch of roses was like consent, like an approval of what she had done. Tonight she would burn all her memories together with the witches and she would go back to her childhood when she was her father's princess. Now she knew she was loved again, she felt as light as a feather, her life would be fulfilled and she would let nobody break this unique connection. Tonight would be the beginning of the end.

Fer's mind absorbed the magic cure like a sponge, the way it should be picked up, so it was not difficult for him to fulfill this ritual. All day long he wandered to pick up the "We the Great." He talked not only to the wind but he kept praying to the Creator to carry this task to the end and learn the magic charm. He did not know how to do it but he felt guided by a force that gave him courage. He felt how he changed himself, how the curing powers of nature grew within him, purified him, bathed his body and soul in the beauty and goodness of the beginning, where there was no pain, suffering, or death. He became a part of the Creator through his faith, he became what he had forgotten to be: A HUMAN BEING.

The heaviest burden that the planet could hold was the people who changed into destroyers, into real beasts, for whom the evil became law, and the laws were made to cover the horrible facts. They took the place of the devil to keep the secrets hidden in the hell of mankind.

Being one with nature, Fer went back to point 0 where kindness and the power of love were the only qualities of people. With these long-forgotten weapons and a strong will, he headed towards the mine just when the sun was setting on the horizon.

Lucy looked into the mirror once again. Her rust-colored hair was spread on her shoulders, her scarlet dress stretched over her body reminded her of a venomous snake in search of prey. Her long black cloak with a hood was the symbol of power, of a supreme judge. Her face expressed nothing but hatred and revenge. Today she would give the sentence she had prepared for. In the morning, she saw Fer leaving on his mysterious walks.

He seemed changed in the way he walked, the way he held his body, as if he carried the burden of the entire world, like a lamb taken to a slaughter-house but at the same time, he was determined. He walked deep in his thoughts, like a sleepwalker, like a remote-controlled doll. He might have been feeling that something was going to happen today, the destiny would be fulfilled. Letting her brother continue his walks, Lucy got dressed and hurried to the mine. She put some sleeping pills in the water that the girls were going to drink so she would not have problems carrying them and tying them up to the funeral piles. As expected, the girls drank the water and she could carry them with no difficulty. They were so light and everything went unexpectedly well. But she had problems with Magi. Even though she was scared, she opposed and tried to tell her how sick she was and that she could help her. With a little effort, Lucy made Magi drink the poison and put her where she belonged. "Tonight, tonight." Lucy kept repeating while going home. "Tonight I shall feel happiness again. One thing bothered her, the fact that Fer was not with her to feel this complete fulfillment. After giving her the roses and the note telling her how much he loved her, her hopes grew higher. She was sure he would approve of her actions and if she asked, he would be next to her because Fer was nobody else but her father. She was not always sure of that, once he was, once he was not, sometimes she seemed to see them both in one. Then she decided it was better to wait till they separated and she remained a simple observer. Until that morning when she received the bunch of roses and the note, she thought that it was Fer who remained. But he would not have written something like that: "A little of how much I wanted to offer you... With love..." There was only one man that could have offered her love and that was her father. All this time, he was with her, he watched her deeds, encouraged her by staying aside and not getting involved. It was a test of decision, courage, and most of all of love. She was sure she had successfully passed the test and what was going to happen tonight would connect them forever. With her face beaming with joy, she looked in the mirror once more, wanting to look perfect while meeting death.

With a face of stone, Lucy stood in front of the funeral piles and admired her work. Suddenly, her mouth opened and she burst into a roar of laughter that flowed like the waves hitting the cliffs and returning again to burst harder. Her body shattered through convulsions under the black cloak as it seemed to blow up like a cliff. This was the end and the little flame in her hand would change into a dance of victory.

Fer reached the mine with his face transfixed with tiredness but feeling that small part of divinity, that miraculous power of nature. The doors were wide open as if somebody had left them that way on purpose, inviting him to come in. Calmly holding the cup with the magic cure, he stepped into the last bit of the way. Lucy's laughter invaded the galleries, moving the dust and making the old wooden beams creak. Staring at Magi, he took the last few steps to the water that separated them. Then he saw her catch power and he heard the magic charm like the river that rushed for the first time from darkness into light. His lips were repeating the words as if it has always been in his mind and heart. He could see the small flame in Lucy's hand, then a big fire caught the whole little island as if swallowing it. With his last powers, he sprinkled her, and then he fell down.

The surprise was so great that for a moment, Lucy remained with the match in her hand. She would have liked to run into her father's arms but the flame burned her finger. She dropped it on the pile of straw that she had prepared and a huge fire started, blinding her for a moment. When she recovered, she saw Fer down on the ground and she was so scared she was not able to move. Drops of sweat were on her forehead, her mouth was dry, and then she rushed to him screaming with grief. She saw a jug of water that smelled appetising and feeling the thirst, she rushed to it and started to drink. The next moment, she felt a splitting headache as if some iron circles were snapping as if the whole cave was spinning in a stunning waltz. She breathed harder and harder, her heart was beating like a steam engine ready to die and her temples were twitching under the blood rush. Her whole body listened to an invisible force that she could not control. She felt the change, a purifying wind swept off all the pain, evil, leaving behind a pure and clean soul.

She could see her life so smoothly, her mother with tears in her eyes and her father smiling happily, finally finding their child from old times. After so many years her soul was at peace. All she wanted was to get out into the fresh air, to listen to the wind and the forest that was preparing to go to sleep, the old trees cracking from all their old joints. She stood in the middle of nature like a newborn child in the water for baptizing.

Still weak from the effort, Fer opened his eyes. Everything was surrounded by smoke. He saw the flames ready to catch the funeral piles and Magi who was scared to death. She was in front of the fire, fighting helplessly to escape. He had no time to reach the ground so he crossed the water but everything was on fire. The only way was through the fire if he wanted to save her. His clothes caught fire, there was a smell of burnt flesh but he was in front of her, untying the ropes.

'I thought you would not make it.'

She said crying and she fell in his arms.

Despite the pain caused by the burns, he held her close to his chest, protecting her from the fire. He took her to the stream of water, put her far from the hell, and went back to untie the other two girls. He was badly burnt but he had no time for himself. He had to keep his promise, a promise he made when he had found them in the mine the first time. He had to take them out of the fire. To his surprise, she had no burn marks. When they were all safe, he felt the life running out of his body and Magi's imploring look and her kiss full of love. He closed his eyes and slipped into oblivion.

Magi was holding his head on her chest, wishing to give her life instead.

'God, if you really love people, if you are good, wise, and forgiving, please forgive our sins and help us see your glory. We are standing hopelessly in front of you but we are full of hope. We trustingly put our lives in your hands and we are waiting for you to make a miracle.'

'If anything has a price, weigh the deeds but please ask for any price and give me another fate because you are the source of life and death.'

Eminescu's lines came to her mind and they matched the end of the prayer perfectly. Then she thought how strange everything was, in another corner of the world, she used the magic charm and now she prayed to the Creator using the lines of the greatest poet of her native country.

The fire was almost over and the girls, despite being only skin and bones, were leaning on one another. They were sitting down next to Magi and were watching helplessly the inert body in her arms. Magi, with closed eyes, was praying continuously and they all united their voices in a murmur full of grief. A piece of wood cracked from time to time throwing sparks like fireworks. A small cloud of smoke wound with its last strength, the small stream of water monotonously buzzed but their whisper was heard like a heart-breaking cry. Finally, Magi opened her eyes, looked up to the sky thankfully, and rose to look for something. She saw the jug of water where Lucy had left it, took it, and sprinkled Fer, moistening his lips with the magic cure. She lay on his body and they became one single being. She knew that she would stand up only with him.

Lucy threw off the black cloak and remained like that in the middle of nature. She ranfrom one tree to another, hugging them, sticking her face on their bark, and caressing them. She listened to the whispers of the night, the soft song of leaves, the chirping of little birds in their nests. She missed the protective arms of her father, the warm and loving smile of her mother, the little, shy and helpless Fer, but she no longer felt the desire to protect anybody or the need for revenge. She felt as light as a flower petal that was let free to run. She was the little girl from old times again, for whom every day was a holiday. Once she arrived in front of the house, she was afraid to enter. She could not give up everything she had but at the same time, she had to accept her deeds. It was the moment of truth, when facing reality she would have to choose, could she live with it or not?

Full of fear, she went upstairs to her room for the last confrontation before death, the choice of the last way, the redemption of the sins. She opened the diary. All her victims rushed into her soul smothering her, squeezing her with the claws of horror and death. Crying and sobbing, she realized how sick she was, how much pain she had caused with her imaginary treason. Neither she nor they deserved such a fate but now it was too late, at least for her.

Uniting with Fer and being a single body, their love defeated death. Life came back to Fer's weak and fragile body like a candle that had just been lit. He opened his eyes but for a moment, everything was confusing. When he saw the three girls bent over him, he remembered the whole nightmare and he knew they were saved.

'I knew, I believed, I prayed and here you are, among us. Thank you for the gift you gave me, it means you exist and you care.'

It was her thanking the Creator before holding him in her arms and giving him her eternal love.

Despite the injuries caused on his head, Fer stood up. The place looked like after the arson, only the smoke struggled to cough, like a dying man in agony. He first thought about Lucy. He did not know what happened after he had fallen but he knew he did not give her the magic cure. He was desperate.

'I know what you are thinking about, it is your sister. The fact that you had fallen before giving her the magic cure.'

She told him all that happened after he had lost consciousness. She saw the color returning to his cheeks and joy invaded his heart. He came closer to her and squeezed her in his arms so hard that she almost lost her breath.

'My darling, I must thank you for everything. It means that Lucy is reborn and our life can be a normal one. Let us hurry and find her to watch the wonder with our own eyes.'

But it was not as easy. The two girls had to be helped because they were powerless. Especially the one in the shaft could not stand up and she could hardly use her legs. He had to carry her in his arms all the way through the mine but the other one walked supported by Magi. Once they were out in the grass full of dew, they let themselves bath in the cool air of the night. The two girls who had thought they would never see the sky again were coming to life minute by minute. They were sitting on the ground with their hands thrust into it, for fear to lose it again. They all needed a moment of relaxation, a new beginning.

'I think it is time we hurried back home and tried to find Lucy. We shall leave the girls near the oak at the edge of the forest until we are sure everything is ok.'

The way back was pretty difficult because they were all weak and full of wounds and the two girls had to be carried. Fer's desire to go faster was so strong that he did not feel the effort. Something was urging him to hurry, he was divided between his desire to see his sister, to break off this spell that had kept them tied for such a long time to a past and present that havd never been his and his desire to be free. All he wanted was to be alone, to have one life he could identify with. Enough with the long midnight walks, with hiding, with simulations, with the fear that somewhere somebody was watching and analysing you. When they reached the oak tree, they saw something sparkling and they got frightened. Downstairs, timidly at first, the flames of fire started to grow and go upstairs. The four of them were shocked watching such a terrible scene. Fer started to run and Magi followed she shouted in vain to stop him. He was trying to find a way to enter the house and save Lucy. She appeared in the window with a smile on her face. She waved to Fer, wanting to say that everything was exactly as she wanted it. Her calm and serene face showed she was pleased and pointing to the car parked out of the fire and she urged him to go there. Fer could not give up his desire of saving her and was looking for a place to sneak in. Suddenly, a strong blow of fire threw him a few meters away from the house while it burned like a funeral pile. Lying down on his back, Fer knew there was nothing else to be done and he felt Magi approach and give him a diary with a sheet of paper annexed to it.

Here you will read what should have never happened. I lived in the darkness but you showed me the way to the light. The power of your love made me see all the evil around me. Do not be sad because they had forgiven me and now they are waiting for me. Now it is your turn to forgive me but as I know you, you will find much compassion and forgiveness in your soul. I loved you before and I will love you after death too. Your sister Liana.

Fer was watching Magi through the tears that were falling from his eyes. There was something scary in that look, something that was paralysing her. She felt a smell of horror, death. She would have wanted to run away and also to rush into his arms and be with him for eternity. They were united by the biggest secret of mankind. Nobody would ever decode this secret, that somebody could die for – LOVE.

THE END

The author

Born in a small city in Romania in 1955, Eleonora
Georgeta Bulz grew up spending her holidays
visiting her grandparents in a small village at the
base of a mountain. She enjoyed the freedom of
roaming the hills, mountains, and forests close by
and spent lots of time connected to nature. She
worked as head of reception and then manageress
in a hotel and thereafter became a care assistant in
a nursing home. After the revolution in Romania in
1989, Bulz was driven by her passion and started
an animal charity. Bulz is divorced and currently
resides in the UK. Her hobbies include saving
animals and writing books, where she draws from
her experiences of living in Romania.

The publisher

He who stops getting better stops being good.

This is the motto of novum publishing, and our focus is on finding new manuscripts, publishing them and offering long-term support to the authors.
Our publishing house was founded in 1997, and since then it has become THE expert for new authors and has won numerous awards.

Our editorial team will peruse each manuscript within a few weeks free of charge and without obligation.

You will find more information about novum publishing and our books on the internet:

w w w . n o v u m - p u b l i s h i n g . c o . u k